PORNO MANIFESTO

By
Kyle Michel Sullivan

Published by: KMSCB, Buffalo, NY

For
Mahmoud Asgari, 16, and Ayaz Marhoni, 18, who were
hanged in Iran for "homosexual acts".
And to the churches and states who support these evil actions,
up yours.

Cover design by Kyle Michel Sullivan
Copyright 2008 by Kyle Michel Sullivan, dba: KMSCB

PORNO MANIFESTO

Table of Contents

One

I know exactly when the thought came to me. And I can tell you for a fact, it was not before I was gay-bashed...at least, not that I can recall. I have to admit my memory is still not a hundred percent. I just know I never used to be the kind of guy who'd sit around contemplating possible reactions to various actions perpetrated against him or that he took. I had a career (I-T Guy) that demanded too much focus for that, and a decent circle of friends and family to entertain and to entertain me (and back me up when I'm not positive about something I used to know). No lover at the moment, but that was more by choice than chance. Or vise-versa, maybe. My hobby (photography) also took a lot of attention, and I never let myself get involved in any political crap (short of voting every election). No, I first came up with my porno manifesto after I was nearly killed, not before like some assholes want to insist, now that everything's come out in the open.

Gay-bashed. That sounds worse than it was. I didn't wind up comatose like that guy in West Hollywood, a few years back. Nor was I killed like that kid near Santa Barbara or something, obviously (and unfortunately, according to a few right-wing freaks). But it was still the most terrifying moment in my almost thirty years of existence, and it would have been worse had I not been taking classes in self-defense. That's not to say I'm good at dropping and rolling and kicking the shit out of my assailant. I'm better at dropping and rolling and getting the hell away from them as they try to figure out what I've just done. And that's basically what happened that Tuesday night in February.

No...that's not right. I was attacked on a Wednesday; it gets hazy, now and then. But it seems to me everything really started the night before. Started so nicely. Who could've known it would wind up like it did?

Tuesday night. I stopped working on this pain-of-a-site for a new client – Wendahl Sportswear – at six-thirty, hit the gym at seven, had a decent dinner of fish and veggies at eight-thirty and hopped into a bar near my townhouse about ten. I intended to quaff one beer and spend twenty minutes flirting with this doll of a bartender I had a crush on...but then I saw Freddy. Dark-haired, dark-eyed, golden-tanned Freddy. A bit shorter than me. A bit heavier in weight. Smooth muscles with just the right amount of softness to keep him human. Good clean lines to his arms and neck. Barely old enough to drink (if he really was). And lips to send you to heaven. He was wearing a T-shirt that was just tight enough and jeans that were just loose enough to add to the curve of his body. I stopped cold the second I saw him, the thoughts of Chad or Greg or whatever the bartender's name was (I used to know it; hell, I used to know a lot of things) shot straight to hell.

Now I'm not the best looking guy in the world; I know that. My shoulders are wide and my legs are long for my body, and I've only recently begun to have some real definition to my own muscles; it took eighteen months in the gym for that to happen. And my face is on the lean side with sharp cheekbones. Plus since I'm blond people have certain expectations of me that I do *not* meet. For example, dumb; I also design and build specialty websites for small businesses and service them. Or party animal; I prefer a beer at dinner with friends to chugging Pina Coladas in a dance bar. I'm not adventurous in bed, preferring kissing and fondling and cuddling to actual sex (tho' there's nothing wrong with it, believe me). And I do *not* have a tan line (knowing perfectly well what the sun does to the skin of Nordic types like me). But my eyes are cool green and intense (my best feature) and I have...had an open smile and a quiet way of talking to hot little beasties like Freddy that could make them think I'm more in control than I really am.

He was sitting alone on a stool at the bar, handing out a "Don't even think about it" vibe that's usually a turn-off to me. That type – when it comes to sex, you have to do the all work while they get all the fun. But this time...this time, it made me more interested, for some reason.

At the time I didn't know why. I sort of thought it was due to the hint of sadness in his eyes. Or the way he focused so intently on his beer (Amstel Light, my favorite). Or the fact that he just plain ignored the gorgeous bartender (I really have to write his name down so I make sure to remember it), which was sacrilege in a gay bar. Whatever it was, I slipped onto a stool two seats down from him, ordered my own Amstel and pulled out a copy of Froissart's "Chronicles." I propped it on the counter, took a sip of my beer and studiously ignored him as I sent hidden glances his way.

I read for about ten minutes, mixing in some chit-chat with Chad/Greg about life and nonsense, before Freddy ordered another Amstel, giving me my in.

"Good choice," I said, acting like I'd just noticed that was what he's drinking.

He shrugged and handed Chad/Greg a five. "It works."

"That doesn't sound good," I said, putting down my book. His only response was to put the fresh beer to his lips and, What I wouldn't give to be that beer bottle, did a flash-frame across my brain, but what I said was, "If all you want to do is get drunk, maybe you should try something stronger."

"Or cheaper. Right."

I shook my head and turned back to my book. He was starting to sound condescending and I don't need that. A guy I was involved with straight out of college was full of the "I'm too cool for you" attitude and I was dumb enough to think I could prove otherwise. I couldn't. No one could. Since him, I'd left the "Ain't-I-perfects" to their self-inflicted solitude – less from a conscious decision to do so and more because the catastrophe of that experience still had me skittish about anything more than a one-nighter.

I finished out my chapter on "The Siege of Calais," bookmarked my page then pulled a twenty from my wallet and motioned to Chad/Greg. He bopped over like a big happy Lab and I let my heart do its usual flip at seeing his way-too-sexy-albeit-totally-manufactured grin.

"Just one, tonight?"

I nodded. "I'm meeting my crew here, tomorrow."

He bopped away to get my change, and I heard, "Wait...you come to a bar to read?" I turned to Freddy with a smile and raised eyebrows, faking like I hadn't heard him. He was looking at me, truly confused. "That book...you're really reading it."

"Yeah."

He looked at the title and frowned. "I never heard of that. What's it about?"

"Oh, medieval times. Pre-Renaissance and The Hundred Years War and all that."

"You a teacher?"

"No, I just like history. It's fascinating to find out where we came from and how our society evolved. A sort of 'learn from the past and you can see the future' kind of thing."

"And you read it for fun? You don't have to?"

You know, it's moments like this that remind me just how weird I can seem to most people...and it always irritates me. So I'm reading a book in a bar? So what? So I like to learn about more than just the latest pop-pop-pop-music trends or gossip crap out of whatever online magazine is hip for the day? You have to make me feel like a dork? I sighed and shot out with, "What can I say?"

Chad/Greg hopped over with my change and I left him a five as a tip. He expected that much just because he was so pretty and lets guys like me flirt with him (I honestly could not tell if he was really gay; the pings on my gay-dar were too laced with self-interest), but I also left it to show Freddy I was more interested in the bartender than in this little twerp who was making me feel out of place.

As I put the rest in my wallet, Freddy took a sip of his beer and said, "You must be smart. A book like that looks like work."

"Only if you want it to be."

"Yeah. Right. Things ain't that simple."

Well...he had me there. But like a smart ass, I just had to ask, "Why not?"

He just looked at me with this cool calculating gaze and shrugged. "Life."

"That's nice and vague."

14

"People."

"And that's relationship trouble."

He nodded. "I just got dumped. Not that we were together all that long...but it still shakes you up."

"Yeah. I've been there. I've also done that."

He looked at me, a hint of confusion in his eyes. I think he was surprised I didn't hand him the usual "How could anybody dump a gorgeous guy like you?" line.

"You dumped somebody?" he asked. And when I nodded, he leaned forward and wondered, "How come?"

Now by this point, I'm starting to see things that make me think he's open to being chased. And caught. Things like how his thumb would trail from his lip to his chin after he took a sip of beer. And how his head would cock (pun NOT intended) at an angle as he looked at me. Oh, I'd have to initiate things and he'd be casual about it for a bit, but something in his sudden interest and basic body language said, "If you wanna..." And I sort of...did.

I smiled and decided to try being quick and bold, for once. "Well – a one night stand is a lot of fun, but sometimes you think it could wind up being more. Then you see each other a couple of times and realize that's how it should have stayed."

He slipped off his stool and turned to lean back against the bar, giving me a perfect view of his perfect body. Full pecs lightly dusted with hair curled into sleek abs that dipped behind jeans riding at just the right position on his hips. His crotch was nice...ripe...and his legs held just the right curve, giving his jeans an even sexier look as they bunched around his gray and red Nikes. Totally hot...and he knew it. And he had every reason to know it. And I deliberately swept my eyes over him to let him know I knew it, too.

He took a sip of his beer and said, "You do that much? One nighters?"

"Only my share."

His smile widened, and it was a lovely smile. "I've never done one," he said, looking away. "It's kind of dangerous."

"And sexy...if you play careful. With the right person." (That reads lamer than it sounded at the time.)

"Don't you think it's better to know the person, first?"

I offered my hand and chimed, "Alec Presslea, at your service."

"That could be taken wrong," he chuckled, then said, "Freddy. What do you do, Alec?"

Not wanting to sound either too rich or too geeky, I said, "Operations manager for Wendahl Sportswear." Which wasn't a total lie; I was trying to finish up the structure of an online catalogue and ordering system for them (and having trouble with it, as noted earlier) but that sort of made me an operations manager. Sort of. Of course, Chad/Greg overheard and gave me a quick glance, but I winked at him and he turned away with a knowing smile.

"I heard of them," said Freddy. "Their stuff looks gay."

"Yeah, it does. We're trying to expand beyond that. Fact is, we just got in our spring line and some of that looks more 'Every-guy' than 'Aber-zombie'."

"Yeah?"

"Yeah. Y'know, I have one of the new catalogs at home. You want to come see?"

He did. And it surprised me how easy it was to get him to come back to my place. Initially I wondered if he was serious or if all he planned to do was scope my place out and come back later to rip me off. Then I thought he was just gonna get me all hot and ready before springing the comment, "You want more, it's two-hundred bucks" or something. Finally I figured he's just out to show his ex that he's still cool enough to get picked up by anybody...and prove it to himself, as well. Not that I cared; I just wanted to get him alone. So we walked the whole three blocks (through a gentrified part of town) and I gave him a tour of my spare-but-stylish-in-an-"Architectural Digest"-kind-of-way cave.

It's funny – I call it a townhouse but really it's just a glorified condo. Steps lead up to an entrance I share with a similar unit on the other side of the building, but I also have the level directly below me, which I use as my office; the other side is a separate apartment. A side entrance leads to stairs and an elevator that take you up to the second floor, where the regular condos begin. Quirky but comfy; suited me perfectly.

16

I won't bore you with the next half-hour's chit-chat and wordplay. Let's just say that after a couple more Amstels, Freddy and I were flopped on my couch, drifting. For some reason, we were listening to an old Depeche Mode CD ("101", I think) and the conversation was at a lull. He was leaning back, his gorgeous legs parted in a casual fashion, his half-gone beer resting on one thigh, his eyes focused on nothing. And I was beside him, looking at his amazing profile (Greek, probably...or northern Italian).

I grew bold, again, and slipped my fingers over his right shoulder. He didn't react...so I let them drift down his arm and across the fabric of his T-shirt. He let a little sigh escape his lips when I drew my thumb over the tit, so I gave it a bit of a pinch...and got a gasp of pleasure as my reward. Then I leaned over and kissed him, long and deep, whispers of the beer mingling with the scent of his skin.

It wasn't the greatest kiss. He seemed to hold back, seemed to be unsure. I didn't care; I let it linger for just long enough...then I proceeded to kiss his cheeks and his chin and his nose and his eyes and his eyebrows and his ears then ran my lips along the line of his jaw and down his throat to tickle the hairs on his chest that peeked over the collar of his T-shirt. My fingers drew soft over his pecs and swirled around his tits and tickled down his sides and over his abs to slip under the soft fabric and glide it up and over his body. Without a word, he lifted his arms and let me remove the shirt and gaze at his tight toned torso.

Just as I expected, his skin was smooth over solid muscles that weren't overdone, like you see in muscle mags or the porn sites. A treasure trail of light hair danced up to his navel and playfully twirled slightly away from the center then tightened, once more, and lead up to a light dusting of hair that flowed out over his chest. His tits were rosy brown ovals, unpierced, firm and ready to be used. And no tattoos (that I could see, anyway).

I let my lips encircle one tit. Let my teeth take hold of it and hold it as my tongue flitted over it. The fingers of my left hand toyed with the other. His breathing quickened and his back arched, and the way he squirmed under my touch let me know he was loving it. I shifted to kneel between his legs, then my fingers slowly drew down his sides and along the top of his jeans to trace down the line of his fly as it bunched over his crotch, then they caressed the inner seam of his jeans before coming to rest on his thighs. I could feel his muscles clench and tighten in reaction, almost quiver, at times. I'd never felt so completely in control.

He hadn't moved yet, not really, just reacted to what I was doing. Little moans escaped from him to let me know I was hitting all the right spots. His body arched a bit more when I shifted from one tit to the other. His hands remained still, letting me do as I wanted but not adding to the moment, and I thought, "No surprises here; just another pretty boy who likes being serviced." I figured I'd make him really go nuts, then.

I let my tongue get to work on the line of hair leading from his chest down his belly...and he gasped, despite himself. I licked his little innie of a belly button as my fingers tickled the backs of his legs and slipped up to his hips.

"Shit," he muttered. "Don't tease."

Your wish is my command, sahib. I slipped my hands around his ass, felt his cheeks clench as I dug my fingers into them and nuzzled my face into his crotch. He smelled salty, a little like peanuts. (It's weird, I know, but that's what I thought of.) He bucked his hips up, ramming his crotch into my face, surprising me. Impatient, I thought.

I undid the button to his jeans...slid down the zipper and pulled the flaps apart to reveal clean white briefs clinging and bulging in all the right places. Too perfect.

I guided his jeans down, pulling the briefs with them a little to expose some of his ass...and he stopped me.

"Don't do that," he murmured. He guided my hands back to his crotch...so I traced my fingers over the rolling seams, instead, and tickled the hairs that peeked from behind the white cotton. He squirmed, his breath quickening. Finally, I pulled the front of the briefs down slowly...slowly...slowly...to reveal inch by inch a nice, neat, ready-to-use dick that let itself be seen completely before it flipped up and over to greet me. It was thick and round, not yet hard but getting there, and had a perfectly shaped pink head that was all but begging my tongue to meet it half way. So I did.

I licked the head then ran my lips down the shaft...and he grew ramrod straight in a nanosecond. Then I pulled back to admire just how perfect he looked – his jeans halfway down his thighs, his briefs gliding around his hips to dip behind balls that hung round and smooth, his dick flopped back, soft dark hair framing his crotch and gliding down his legs. Then I slipped my lips over the head and down the shaft and I pumped sweet little Freddy for everything he was worth, my left fingers rolling his balls against each other and my right ones caressing the hairs along the inside of his thighs.

Oh, he loved it. His hips ground his dick into my mouth. His perfect ass tightened and shoved and shifted away from my groping hands. His beautiful round balls bounced slightly as he tried to hump my throat. The feel of it all – it was right. Almost too right.

He came quickly. Cried out as he grabbed my hair and rammed himself into my mouth and unloaded. I gently twisted both his tits and kept working him for every ounce of juice he had, kept him going until he was so rock hard, he was bout to pop. He finally whimpered, "Don't tease," and pulled himself away. And then he just lay there, looking straight ahead, breathing deep, his jeans loose around his knees, his briefs halfway down his thighs, his beautiful dick growing soft and lying happy atop his groin, and his perfect balls hanging loose between his legs. God, I wanted to take a picture of him like that, it was so erotic.

I didn't swallow. Never have. I just smiled and let his semen spill from my mouth into a bandana I had, then I leaned in to nuzzle his crotch, hoping he'd relent and let me explore his just right ass. Get some of my own jollies (if you know what I mean). After all, I wasn't exactly satisfied. My own nice average dick was ripe and ready for Freddy.

But instead of reciprocating, he suddenly stood and yanked his briefs and jeans back up. He was buttoned up and tucked in with his shirt back in place before I could think of anything to say except, "Uh, Freddy..."

"Gotta go, man. Got a class in the morning. Thanks for the beer...and stuff."

And bam – he vanished out the front door.

I just sat there, confused, and finished off my Amstel. I hadn't even gotten his phone number or address in case he wanted a repeat...which I figured meant he didn't. Too bad. I would have liked one. And to be honest, I felt he owed me a little more exploring time. Or at least a couple of artsy poses for my camera and personal jack-off moments. But I figured he was just one of those straight boys who need nothing more than to get their rocks off and knew that a fag was an easy blow job. After all, he'd been pretty careful about mentioning whether a man or a woman had dumped him. Didn't matter. At least I'd gotten a little something out of the deal, so I went to bed happy.

The next night...well, at just before one the following morning (no...no, it was earlier...before eleven), as I headed back home from the bar, deep in self-disgust and maniacally comparing Freddy and his all around beauty to an ex of mine, I was jumped by five guys. And that started my descent into hell.

Two

Until that night, I'd never really thought about how much we live our lives in hope. Not so much for blockbuster dreams like winning the lottery (everybody's aware of those), but just for having your day progress in a linear fashion. Like being able to drive to work without being hit by a truck. And believing your coffee will be in a clean cup and the sandwich you buy at the local Mom-And-Pop won't be two days older than it should be. Ridiculous things you never pay attention to...until the order of your existence is shattered and you have to figure out how to put the pieces back together. Sometimes, even when you can reconstruct your life, bits stay missing that keep everything out of whack.

That's how it was for me. All day I'd gone through my usual routine – wake at seven am, read the paper over juice and fruit, dress (since I'm a night shower person), and start work, believing subconsciously that everything would be in order. Granted, my work wasn't exactly a nine-to-five sort of thing. Some days I could get everything done that I needed to get done in a space of two hours; other days I'd labor sixteen to twenty hours straight to get a plan completed on time. That Wednesday, I'd done as much as I could by four-thirty.

I met some friends at "Caruso's" for dinner about seven. It was my buddy Lonnie's birthday and six of us were giving him a surprise party. We'd arranged a five course Italian meal then planned to meet some more people at Chad/Greg's bar for drinks. We also got Lonnie one great big gift instead of a bunch of cheap-assed ones. One older guy – Willis, whom I didn't know too well (he and a tall thin buddy of mine named Steubin had been an item for a few months) – suggested we buy an escort for Lonnie's enjoyment...but no one else felt it was right. Thank God. We asked Tad, a sleek guy in the group who was a jewelry salesman on Clarion Street (very high-class), to get us a deal on a Rolex and we all chipped in. It was perfect...ten times better than foisting our buddy on some poor unsuspecting dude who was just trying to work his way through college or a drug habit – or both.

Now don't get me wrong; I think Lonnie's a great guy. He's a year older than me, he says (I think it's really closer to five), and a marathoner who goes into withdrawal if he doesn't run at least an hour each morning, so he's in top shape. In fact, he's the reason I keep working out. I'd tried the gym thing before, but Lonnie's encouragement was what prevented my giving it up after a few months of getting nowhere, this time. "It takes an average of a month of exercise for every year you've been out of shape to get into shape, Alec. You've got years of work ahead of you." The bitch – though I'd laughed when he said it because I knew it came from love. So I'd kept at it. And I was finally glad I had.

But Lonnie also had this streak of...I dunno...fury in him that drew him to dabble in the darker side of life. Meaning some really kinky sex. Bondage and uniforms and such, things which made me uncomfortable. So we'd stayed friends and casually avoided becoming lovers; I think I was too white bread for him and he figured vise versa on my part.

Anyway, the evening went just right. Lonnie was surprised and loved his gift and we ate too much and drank too much wine and slammed into the bar about ten, en masse. Chad/Greg saw us coming and pulled out a bottle of decent Cabernet. One of the crew we were meeting there had given him the heads up about where we were eating (I think it was Joseph, another programmer who was closer to what you'd think a computer geek looks like, but in a cute, sweet, Jewish guy kind of way).

"This'll keep you away from the hard stuff," he said. "We don't want anybody hitting the floor, tonight."

I felt bold because of the wine (and my success with Freddy, the night before) so I patted Chad/Greg's face and said, "I always knew you loved me."

He just grinned and poured each of us a glass. And I watched his beautiful hands as he did it. Long, amazingly expressive fingers curled around the neck of the bottle. Nails manicured to just the right length. I was fascinated by how right his thumbs looked...how they matched the whole feel of his hands as he worked. I think I sighed...and that's when Lonnie jabbed me in the arm.

"Aren't we the greedy guts?" he said.

I looked at him, confused, and asked, "Do you mean anything by that?"

"I hear you took home a hot little number, last night. And you never breathed a word to me."

I shrugged. "He wasn't that hot. And he split so quick, I can't even say for sure he was there."

"You still got some, didn't you?"

"No, Lonnie, he got some. All I got was my right hand."

Lonnie smirked. "Typical. But it's beside the point. It's not polite to also want the only guy in here who's worth prison, not after getting yourself a pretty straight boy."

"'Worth prison?' Your phrases are built to confuse."

"It means our favorite bartender's worth committing a crime to get." I must have looked even more clueless, so he added, "Date rape drugs. Forcible bondage. You know, felonies. A few of my favorite things."

"Except, obviously, you will never be Julie Andrews."

"I might as well be a nun, right now." I gave him another confused look and he let out with one of his patented deep sighs, the kind that seems to rise up from his toes. "I'm going through a dry spell, hence the green eyes when I heard Mr. Green Eyes made a conquest."

"Maybe we *should* have bought you a stud instead of a watch."

Lonnie glanced at me, a little pissed. "Don't you even *think* about suggesting that. When the day comes that I can't pick up a guy, I'll cut my dick off."

"Get one tonight. There's some cute beasties in here."

"I don't believe it. Alec The Angel is suggesting I prowl for a pick-up?"

"Yeah, soon I'll begin dipping into the blackness of life's evil relationships. Maybe I'll even pick up Chris."

(CHRIS! That's Chad/Greg's name. Jeez, what's wrong with my brain?)

"Forget it, honey," said Lonnie. "I think he's straight. Just not narrow."

Now maybe it was the wine taking over. I'd had about three glasses too many and I glanced down to notice my fourth glass too many was now empty, and I wanted to make that five glasses over my limit. Whatever it was, I sneered at Lonnie and said, "Watch your angel turn a little devilish."

I motioned for Chris to refill my glass. He gave me a look as if to say, "I dunno..." but I held up a twenty and kept waving, so over he came with a fresh bottle.

"You're really celebrating, tonight, Alec," he said as he poured in half a glass.

"I'm starting a whole new life," I said. "A whole new way of viewing the world. Caveat emptor!"

"Let the buyer beware?" Chris asked, trying not to smile too much.

"No...uh...e pluribus unum?"

"I think you're really gonna regret this in the morning."

Lonnie smirked, beside me, irritating me even more, so I turned to Chris and blurted out, "The only thing I'll regret in the morning is not taking you home, tonight."

Chris smiled his killer smile, took the twenty and turned to the register to make change, shaking his head the whole time. He thought I was playing. But when he turned around, I had a fifty in my hand.

"I mean it," I said.

Chris' smile froze in place.

"You're drunk," he snapped. "You're not getting another one of these."

Man, that jolted me out of my cockiness. I crumpled the fifty into the palm of my hand and stood up straight, saying, "Chris, I'm sorry. I...I was just joking, man."

"Yeah. Right. I know."

He slapped my change on the counter and headed down to the other end of the bar.

Lonnie hadn't moved, but I could just hear him thinking, "That was one of your less brilliant moves."

24

My head started to swim, not just from the wine but from the understanding of what I'd just done. And so friggin' clumsily, too. But I have this way of dropping into a mind-set that makes me cocky and sure and lets me think I know what I'm doing...and then suddenly I wind up with foot-in-mouth or face-in-mud. It's like a glitch in my character that says, "I've got to screw up once in a while to keep from becoming too sure of myself." And here it was – my time of month and I'd just fucked up my one-way near-friendship with Chris. What a fuckin' idiot.

I bolted for the door, leaving Lonnie behind. I heard him calling, "Alec, don't! C'mon, it's not that big a deal!" But I slammed outside and headed for home.

It was chilly out (no, it was February and it was fucking cold) and I'd left my coat in the bar, but I couldn't go back in there. Not just then. So I just dug my hands into my pants pockets and rushed down the street. It was only three blocks. Three long tedious blocks. Blocks I knew like the back of my hand and which had nothing on them to distract me from my killer thoughts. From trying to figure out why the hell I had done what I just did.

I knew what Chris meant. I'd treated him like a whore. Five dollars for a smile. Fifty to cop a feel. A hundred to let me blow you. It's all the same thing to a guy who's got respect for himself. "Here's some cash; let me have some of you and fuck your self-esteem." Whether I was doing it to be cute or for real meant nothing; I was viewing him as a product for purchase and he'd been insulted. Hell, I'd have been insulted.

Well...no, I wouldn't have. Not once upon a time. Like when I was in college and immediately after. I had negative self-respect. One of the glories of living with an alcoholic mother and two-fisted then absent father. Any guy who wanted me in any way I went with, thinking it was all I was worth. It's funny that I have the persona of being "Mr. Vanilla Ice Cream" now. That I prefer to cuddle with a man instead of fuck with him. It was more of a perverse reaction to what I'd let myself go through after than a real personal preference.

Oh, nobody raped me or beat me or forced drugs down my throat. I just got involved with assholes because I

25

thought that's what I was supposed to do, and a couple got me to do things I still cannot really understand how I...I could do them.

The worst of that group was Woody, my "I'm-too-cool-for-you Fool." Allan Woodrow, actually, but he hated his first name. A bit shorter than me. Stockier. Ten years my senior. And with a strut like an angry tomcat on the prowl that made his to-die-for legs sexier than should be allowed by law. Even though he worked out two or three hours a day, somehow he managed to stay lean and mean and too full of energy instead of turning into the incredible bulk. He had black wavy hair and eyes so dark you could vanish into them. And his lips were made for perfect kisses. But he loved to fuck with you...and I don't mean that in a nice way. What I *do* mean is, he was just my type.

I met him the second time I joined a gym (he was a personal trainer there) and he showed me how to best use the equipment. I got three sessions with him for free; after that, they were sixty bucks each. I was just getting started in my career so I didn't have the cash for it, but I noticed Woody still kept wandering by when I worked out to offer tips. He usually wore tight sweats that accentuated his too-beautiful-for-words body, and I wasn't what you'd call subtle in my notice of it...I mean, when no one else was around to notice I was noticing.

To make a long story short (one that took place over the space of nearly two months), one day I got a charley horse in a calf in the middle of my cardio, and I went limping back to my locker. Woody noticed and followed me.

"Muscle seize up?" he asked as I sat by my locker. I just nodded, so he squatted before me and took my leg and began kneading my calf. "Oh, yeah. This is a mean one."

I almost screamed from the pain of it. He chuckled. That should have told me something.

"Let's hit the massage room and I'll work it out," he said.

I just shook my head. "I think I'll try the Jacuzzi, first."

He stood and took my arm. "C'mon, Alec, I got an ointment that'll cut the pain. It'll work lots faster."

I let him drag me into a tiny room with nothing but a tall padded bench and table topped with bottles of lineaments, and no windows, just a door. I lay on the bench, still in pain, and he closed the door and set the lights to dim.

"Face down," he said. "Gives me access to the muscle."

I rolled over. Gladly. Just having him rub my leg in the locker room had given me a hint of a woody (pun intended), despite the pain. He had good hands, too. Strong. Well shaped. Light wisps of dark hair dancing over his skin. I knew the second my leg stopped hurting, my dick would be raging from his touch. I was so happy I wore briefs.

He slopped some cold lineament on my calf and started kneading it, again...and he was right – the ointment combined with his fingers rolling into my skin and his palms rubbing around my muscle made the hurt vanish. The one and only time he ever did that for me – killed the pain, I mean.

"Wow," was all I could say.

"Yeah. Helps to know what you're doing. I'm surprised you haven't had one of these before now."

"I have. I just walked them off."

"You could keep 'em from happening if you stretched more and had a massage every now and then."

"I'm too broke, right now," I muttered, finally getting into the rhythm of his massage. "I can barely afford the gym."

"Been there. Done that. Lemme check something." Then his hands shifted to the back of my thighs, one on each of them. His fingers played harsh on my skin, digging deep in a way that was guaranteed to make my dick hard as a rock. "Yeah, you're getting tight here, too."

"I...I'll get back to stretching," I muttered, not sure exactly what the hell was happening...other than the fact that every motion of his fingers was sending explosions through every nerve in my body and every damned one of those nerves was suddenly hard-wired straight to my crotch. He had me so on edge, even the slightest movement of my long loose shorts across the hair on my legs was setting off little jolts.

Then his hands shifted to my butt, the kneading motion rubbing the fabric of my shorts against the fabric of my briefs, which rubbed against my scrotum...which was now on fire.

"Hmph," he said, "firmer than I thought. Not bad."

I looked at him, startled. He smiled.

27

"Looks like I'll have to make the first move," he said...then leaned down and kissed me. And, dear GOD, what a kiss. It was the whisper of peppermint drifting from moistened lips. It was warmth of the sort you dream of at home, glowing and cool like the energy of existence. It was the passing of life along conduits made of nature's purest gold. His lips gently melted into mine as his chin and nose caressed mine and heaven seemed to open for a moment.

God, Himself, couldn't have told me that what happened next was wrong, it felt so normal and natural and honest and real. He slipped his hand under my left hip and guided me onto my back, his lips still a part of mine, then his fingers trailed over my stomach and down to play with my crotch. He fondled my balls and slipped his hand along my dick, checking the size and weight of it.

"Not bad," he whispered, breaking away from the kiss. Then he gave my dick a squeeze that almost made me explode. "Not so fast." Then he shifted my shirt up and his lips and tongue played over my chin and down my throat and across my chest to toy first with one tit and then the other, his hands slipping under the elastic of my shorts to shift them down my hips.

I was blank. Could not think of a thing to say. Couldn't even think about thinking. To have this perfect-looking man come on to me and now being close to servicing me with no attempt on my part to get him to do it was way out of my sphere of existence. Suddenly, I was nothing but nerve ends dancing with pleasure at his fingers touching me and his lips trailing over me and his tongue tickling me and his chin playing with what little hair I had on my torso. When he finally pulled my shorts and briefs away from my hips, my dick leapt back onto my abdomen, as if to say "Take me, I'm yours!" (A bit Clara Bow-ish, but way too true.)

He pulled back and looked at me and smiled. "No, not bad at all. And a natural blond, to boot."

I was still speechless, so he just leaned in, took me in his mouth and began to run that beautiful velvet tongue along me as the fingers of his left hand played with my balls and the fingers of his right hand played with my ass.

Now, none of this was new to me. I'd been used in the same way by several older men...and I do mean older. An

28

English professor with twenty years tenure. A doctor who started his practice before I was born. One of my dad's business partners, a guy with five daughters (dad almost killed him when he found out, though it was more because he believed the guy was screwing me just to screw pop). But Woody was my first porno-beauty – no, porno-God. And he was porno-good at knowing what to do. I was about five seconds from losing control and firing away when he pulled back.

"Not so fast," he whispered as he slowly guided my shorts and briefs down to my ankles. He played with me for a moment longer, then pulled off his shirt to reveal he looked exactly like I'd known he would – washboard abs under a rich chest behind feathery hair that seemed combed to perfection. Then he lowered his pants to his knees...and I saw he was wearing a jock. I was so startled at seeing it that I laughed.

"What?" he asked then motioned to the jock strap. "This?"

"Sorry," I muttered, trying not to laugh, again. "I just didn't realize non-porn people really used those..."

"Shh."

He pulled it aside to let his own dick stand free...and it was lovely. As rich and full and perfect as the rest of him. Then he ran his hands over my thighs...and over my still hard dick...and around to cup my ass...and suddenly he yanked me down the table to the edge, almost ramming my butt against his crotch. My legs wound up on his shoulders, my shorts behind his head, sort of binding me in position. I gasped at how easy it was for him.

I started to speak, but he shook his head. "Shh." Then he let his dick glide up between my balls and over my pubes to rub along the side of my own...and his fingers pinched at my tits, sending the screams of joy flashing across every nerve in my body, again. He was bigger than me in every way...and more than ready. He pulled back, drawing his dick back down over my balls and then, in the space of a nano-second, his fingers found my anus and he guided his dick to it...and slammed himself inside me. Literally.

I cried out in pain. He put a hand over my mouth and whispered, "Shh," again, then he began to pound away. It hurt like hell...but it also felt so...so fucking erotic that I had to let

29

him have at it, gasping and grunting at the intensity of the experience. And within moments, the hurt was gone and I was clenching at his dick with my glutes. His hand left my mouth and began stroking me...then pumping me as he got close to completion. I came before he did, bucking against him with involuntary spasms as I spewed hard enough to splash cum on my face.

He laughed and then he was firing his own load inside me, over and over and over, until he collapsed atop me, my legs still over his shoulders, his dick still inside me. He kept laughing, softly, even as he lay there, his hands coiled around my ass, his face on my chest, breathing deep and happy. He even nuzzled my abs and licked at some of the cum on them.

Finally, he looked up at me, his face glistening from sweat and semen. Then he grinned and asked, "How's that charley horse?"

I just laughed. And he laughed with me. And we started seeing each other that weekend. And what hell it became.

And that's what I was thinking as I neared my condo. I was remembering Woody and how beautiful he was, at first...and then I realized in one of those blinding flashes of recognition at just how stupid you've been that Freddie had looked a bit like him. As had just about every other guy I'd been involved with since him. And then I saw how Chris did NOT look like him...did not act like him or seem like him, and for that reason I'd tried to treat him like a whore to prove he was really on the same level as me...except that he wasn't.

I was really deep in my confusion, trying to understand why my I hadn't noticed the resemblance between Freddy and Woody, when I heard tires screech, behind me, and somebody yell, "There! Him!" I turned, automatically, and saw a black Ford Bronco stopped in the street and five guys in various kinds of caps jumping from inside it. I had no idea what they were doing...no concept that they were after anything but getting out of that car until one swung at me with a baseball bat. The only thing that kept it from connecting sharp against my temple was I twisted my ankle and fell, so it glanced off my hard head instead of crushing it.

I hit the ground and rolled, without thinking, and started yelling at the top of my lungs. But that didn't stop the guys from piling onto me and punching me and kicking me with grunts and snarls and laughter. And I wondered, for a moment, if this was how I was going to die.

Three

I didn't feel any pain. At least, I don't remember feeling any. I was too pumped on adrenaline to understand how much I was being damaged. I did notice they weren't very organized about the attack. Two of guys flailed at me like wild little monkeys, so busy trying to hit they weren't really getting any done – hell, one never even landed a serious punch, though one still had that baseball bat and was trying to get at me with it.

I rolled back from them and wound up between two cars parked in the street. I like to think I scrambled there, deliberately, but I don't remember it being a conscious decision. It was just a defensive move, meant to give me the rear of one car to half hide under and protect my head and some of my body. All I know is, suddenly I was on my back kicking at the guys as they tried to pull me back onto the sidewalk to pummel me, some more.

I remember the baseball bat bouncing off my left shin and crying out from it. I recall slamming one of my attackers in the ankle with my other foot so hard he cried out from it and limped back. Oh, and I tore one character's shirt as I fell, winding up with a shred of navy cotton in one hand. Then they heard people yelling at them from down the street and backed away.

Suddenly, they were all piling back into the Bronco, its driver screaming, "Come on," and everything was the chaos of athletic shoes topped by jeans hopping into the cabin (except for this one guy in board shorts and deck shoes). I managed to catch a flash of the driver's sneakers – gray Nikes that looked like they had a line of tiny red lights trimming them – before they raced away.

I never heard the people yelling at them, not until they were gone and suddenly Lonnie and Joseph and a couple of guys I didn't know were huddled around me, helping me from between the cars, guiding me to some nearby steps and sitting me down.

"I called 9-1-1," said Lonnie, over and over, punctuating his nervousness with a few, "Motherfuckers."

Joseph was kneeling before me, muttering, "Christ, Alec, there's blood everywhere. You feel dizzy? Sick?"

No, I felt brutally embarrassed. I hated being the center of everyone's attention, as if I'd done something wrong, as if I wasn't deserving of their concern. It's weird, I know...but it's also really how I felt.

So I said, "I'm fine." Again and again and again and again, hoping they'd all go away and leave me alone.

"Bullshit," Lonnie snapped. "Those little fuckers almost killed you. I saw one with a baseball bat. A fuckin' baseball bat! Like this is Texas or fuckin' Arizona!"

Which was not helping me in any way – him saying that, I mean. Emphasizing just how close to death I'd been. More people were gathering around. Lights were coming on in people's windows. Cars slowed down as they passed. And I just wanted to leave (God, I wanted to leave), wanted to pretend it hadn't happened. But when I tried to stand, Lonnie would push me back down.

"Dammit, Alec, sit still!" he snarled, and I could tell from the tone in his voice that he was near hysterics, so I sat. Lonnie's hard enough to handle when he's cool, calm and collected; no way was I going to make him crazier than he already was at that moment.

Joseph, however, was nice and casual.

"Paramedics're coming. Better if you don't move." It amazed me at how easy he was in this situation. I'd never paid much attention to him, before now. He was slim with nice dark eyes...but he was also far too low-key for my taste, too considerate and concerned. Meaning he usually sat around and watched everybody else get drunk and then drove people home, all very quiet and polite. On the rare occasions where I did engage him in conversation, he talked about off-the-wall things like Kierkegaard and his influence on "The Matrix." And how having a brown wallet was indicative of stability while having a black wallet meant you carried deep anger and angst or something (for the record, mine's gray; never did find out what that meant). But here he was, the gentle eye around which the storm of Lonnie circled. I felt blessed.

I heard a siren abruptly stop. I looked up to find two blue and white uniforms bolting from it and I remember thinking, "Wow, were they waiting around the corner?"

One knelt before me, a chunky woman with kind eyes, and she started asking me something...but I couldn't understand a word she was saying. Like her accent was too thick for me to make out English words or phrases or meaning. But Joseph understood her. Hell, he started talking in the same language as her and that was so cool. And I watched him...watched his profile flash and glow as the emergency lights flickered behind him. A nice profile. Clean and classical. Highlights of red and white and blue dancing over his short, dark hair. He kept talking and I kept not understanding, but I had to be polite (one of the few things my mother had drilled into me with too much precision), so I smiled, I think, and said, "Joseph...I didn't know you were bilingual."

And his big dark eyes looked at me, confused.

Next thing I knew, I was in this blinding green and white emergency room, staring at some lights as all these weird people in soft blue uniforms huddled over me, white masks covering the lower part of their faces. I think I giggled and said something like, "Is this an alien abduction? Am I being probed?"

One of the aliens with nice eyes winked at me and said, "Not yet."

And then I was in a hospital room, buzzed on some kind of drug (darvocet or codine, I think; yeah...the vicodin came later) with this steady dull throbbing behind my eyes. And my mouth was as dry as Death Valley, with some kind of grit coating my teeth and tongue and a brutal need to pee threatening my sanitation. And while I had a vague notion of there being a bathroom nearby (I was aware of my surroundings...sort of), I was feeling way too lazy to do anything about any of it. So I lay there. Drifted. Waited for the dull throb to cease.

I vaguely remembered dreaming about someone.

34

Lonnie? Chris? Woody? Their faces sort of jumbled together and seemed to be all of them, at one time...but it didn't seem right. Was it Joseph? Sweet semi-nerdy Joseph? No, the dream was too pleasurable for me and the beauty of my partner was too intense for him to be anything but a porno-God. Open fields cut through by a brook. Thick trees offering shelter from a bright sun. A sky plain and blue and hot. And that perfect someone lying beside me, holding me like no one has, in years. Both of us dressed in white and tan and seeming like two princes from a faux-butter commercial. Him kissing me without any effort on my part. Him touching me without my asking him to. His fingers gliding up my thigh, sending tingles of joy to my heart. His heart becoming one with mine as his hand guided me into nirvana. Gliding up and down and up and down until a bluebird – no, a blue jay perched on my knee and said something weird like, "Hay is for horses." If I remembered right; I couldn't be sure.

What I was sure of is a stirring in my groin, whispering along my thighs in a warm gentle soothing way. It took me a moment to realize I was, for the first time since I was seven, wetting the bed. And it burned. I jolted upright and squeezed off the flow an instant before this sledgehammer slammed against my skull and sent me reeling, and I gave up trying to stop anything. I grunted...no, I probably screamed from the pain, because a nurse popped her head in, her eyes cool as steel.

"He's conscious," she chirped. "And he's got a bad one."

And wouldn't you know it – *that* is when this amazing clone of a gorgeous TV doctor named Doug arrived to check on me. Hey, I may have been on death's door, but I could still notice and very much appreciate male beauty when I saw it – and he was fucking gorgeous.

"Well, well, well, Alec," he chimed. "Welcome back to reality. Now tell me, are you aware that you removed your catheter, and you are now sitting in a pond of pee?"

Before I could even think about it, I did something I'd never done before – I snapped, "No, I think I'm fuckin' water-skiing, dipshit," to a totally hot guy.

Understand, normally when I meet a man I think is gorgeous (and Doug-deux was hot-hot-hot, without question,

35

in that dark-eyed-dark-haired way that I love), I bend over backwards to be nice to him. Say cool casual things to let him know I'm interested if he is, while seemingly just being a buddy. Make low-key conversation about nothing that is meant to lead straight to bed. Didn't matter if he was gay or curious or honed in strictly on chickie-poos (I got more than one straight boy onto the sheets), my act was always the same – My GOD, but you are the MOST interesting man I've ever met in my LIFE! No matter what. But the last few days, (starting with Freddy, to be exact) I'd been stepping out of my usual manners and popping off comments intended to get me nowhere...intended solely to screw me up. And I'd done it, again – though this time the idea it was a dumb move on my part didn't arrive as instantaneously as usual.

Doug-deux blinked and gave me a careful look as he said, "Well, we're not in the best of moods, are we, Alec?"

No, is what I would have said, before, coupled with, I'm sorry. Instead, I snarled, "It's Mister Presslea, Dr – ."

"Danovich, Mr. Presslea," he said, his voice a LOT cooler than before. "And the reason I asked you if you knew what happened is, you've been unconscious for the last four hours and I wanted to know if you're experiencing any disorientation."

"I don't know," I said, still edgy. "My fucking head hurts too fucking much."

Doug-deux smiled and nodded. "Nurse is getting something for that."

"Where'd she fucking go for it? Tibet?"

He got this concerned look on his face and tried to look into my eyes. "Y'know, your friends say you're a nice, quiet guy."

Zing! Away went the fury. And replacing it for the evening? Complete and total self-flagellation, two minutes late and twice as bad. I bunched up and felt myself losing it as I said, "No, I'm an asshole. A fucking asshole." And I started to cry, which made my head scream even louder.

"Okay..." said Doug-deux, "first we're going to get you a clean bed and new gown, then we're going to do a few tests. I assume this is not your normal behavior."

"What the fuck *is* normal behavior?" I blubbered.

"Whatever I say it is," he grinned, back in his good

humor.

The nurse swung in with a syringe and slammed some clear fluid into my I-V as two more uniforms (probably grunts from housekeeping who got paid eight bucks an hour to mop up my pee) rolled a gurney in and put it beside me. The painkiller started working before I was even moved. Then I was cleaned and changed and slapped onto a gurney like a newborn babe into a stroller, and they wheeled me out under the beautiful, dark, snickering eyes of Dr. Danovich.

To make a long story short, I was in the hospital another day and underwent a battery of tests to make sure I wasn't about to have a stroke or had already suffered brain damage. And aside from the dull, soft, never-ending ache behind my eyes, that's basically how everything turned out. Minor concussion, two cracked ribs, a cracked shin, scrapes, bruises, one black eye – I got off easy. Physically. Ran up close to twenty thousand in bills, of which my insurance covered two-thirds; MasterCard and Visa did the rest.

I got a call from my mom (drunk, as usual, so it only lasted two minutes), and Lonnie came to visit me while I was in, bringing a card signed by everyone I knew (including Chris), but it was Joseph who made time to take me home. And while Lonnie and I talked about everything under the sun – like how he'd finally broken his dry spell with the male paramedic who'd tended to me ("Loves to be tied to a dining chair!"), and how Steubin and Willis had a huge argument at the bar ("I thought they were gonna kill each other!"), and how he was the one who first saw the little bastards attacking me and had run back to the bar for help – it was Joseph who asked me if the police had come by.

They hadn't.

"I wondered if they would," he said as we were driving back to my condo. "The patrolmen who finally showed up were more interested in making what happened seem like a mugging than in finding out who did it."

"Maybe it was," I said, trying not to think about it.

"You really believe that?"

"I don't know. No. I don't. I just...I can't..."

Joseph glanced at me and patted my knee. "I understand."

I just looked away and gave my mind permission to

drift. I thought, Joseph said that – did that like a father does with a child. Or maybe like a priest does with an altar boy. Not that I'd know, not being Catholic. And Jewish guys don't have priests to worry about, do they? Just Rabbis. God's chosen people. That's a raw deal if ever there was one and...and maybe that's why I've always had this vague thing for Jewish guys. They're the ones who got fucked. Like me. But then again...I was interested in that type long before I'd put any thought into it. Dunno why, but seeing a guy like...oh, what's his name? The guy on that sit-com..."Ross"...anyway, seeing him on television stops me cold, every time. Big dark eyes. Sweet shy smile. Tall solid build...maybe not a Greek God, but in good proportion. Nice hands. Hangdog gaze. Gentle disposition. Why can't I get a guy like that? Somebody tall and dark and semi-perfect to hold? Somebody to comfort when they're down. To undress slowly, revealing their beauty inch by inch? I've dreamed of that so many times. Wished and hoped and prayed. I could live my life with someone like that. Welcome him home. Fix him a drink. Rub his shoulders as he told me of his day. Nuzzle my nose into his hair. Smell the V-O 5. No...what was it my dad used to use? "Rose Cream?" Made his thick black hair stand up, even in a crew cut. God, I wanted to caress the back of his neck with my lips. Circle his body with my arms. Run my fingers over his belly. Feel the smooth brown skin quiver under my touch. Toy with his full round tits. Fondle his ripe bursting crotch. Hold his big beautiful dick in my hands and squeeze and pull and throw him across the couch and shove his legs apart and yank his pants down and fuck him and fuck him and fuck him hard, like the motherfucker he is and he deserves and would love even though I hated him as mush as he hated – .

    "Alec?"

    Joseph's voice jerked me back from a thousand miles away.

    "You started breathing really fast," he said. "Are you all right?"

    I nodded. Why, I don't know. I had zero understanding of what he was talking about. In fact, I don't think I could have formulated the mental or physical ability to understand anything at that moment, I was so confused. No, disoriented, like when I thought he was speaking another language with the female paramedic.

"Did you hear what I said? About the detective I spoke with? How I have his number?"

All I still could do was nod, even though I hadn't heard a word.

"You don't have to call him, right away. He said they had some leads, already, on your case. But you will need to call him. Tell him what happened. Okay?"

"Yeah," I croaked, my brain still swimming. "In a day or two. Lemme have the number."

Then I looked around and saw we were double-parked in front of my condo. When did we get there? And how long ago? I somehow found the ability to open the passenger door and step out of the car. Joseph stopped me.

"Here." He offered me a slip of paper. "It's Detective Narden's info." I took it. "Now I'll come in with you."

He started to get out. That snapped me back to reality.

"No, Joseph, you're gonna get a ticket."

"Alec..."

"I'll be fine. Really. And I'll – I'll call Detective Narden. In a day or two."

"You sure?"

"Positive."

"Well...okay. You got your painkillers?"

"In my pocket. Thank you so much for bringing me home."

"Alec...c'mon...you'd do the same for me."

Would I? I don't know. Not even now, after all that's happened. After all he's done for me. I honestly could not tell you for sure that I would have been as good a friend to him as he was to me, those few days.

"Thanks, again." Then I turned and headed for the door.

I could feel Joseph watching me as I entered my condo. Could sense the concern in his eyes. I didn't hear his car leave before the door closed, so he may have still have been standing there, making sure I actually made it inside. But I did...and then I stopped moving. Completely. I just stood in the foyer, unable to understand why or who or where I was.

Somewhere...somehow...something deep inside me had shifted. Changed me. How much, I didn't know yet; I still don't know the whole of it. But in a vague sort of misty way I could tell I was different. And this may sound weird, but I think my home sensed it, as well. And it held me in stasis while it tried to make sure I was who I claimed to be. And so I stood there and waited for it to respond as if waiting for my fate.

The sun drew down the sky. Light filtered through the living room windows and caught a crystal object, shooting tiny rainbows into the foyer. One glanced off a mirror I had hanging on a wall and wound up dancing on my cheek. I knew what the object was (a teardrop cut prism hanging from a floor lamp). It was like my home was saying, Okay, you may come in, now.

I shifted. Moved into the living room. Aimed straight for the pendant. It glimmered at me, seemed happy to see me. I took it in my hand and held it up for the sun to catch...and it sparkled and sent joyous prisms of color flying across the dark paint and tasteful furniture. I could almost hear the walls singing, "You're back! Welcome back!" And it really pissed me off, so I dropped the teardrop prism into a trash bin.

Nothing...absolutely nothing was ever going to even seem to give me permission to come into my own fucking house. Nothing. In fact, I didn't need anybody's fucking permission for anything, ever again. From now on, they fucking needed mine.

Four

The next morning I got straight to work and finished
the Wendahl project in the space of two days. Seems getting
my head knocked around helped me realized I was being too
insistent on linking way too many sub-categories with way too
many uber-categories in an attempt to differentiate – well, I
was just making a simple site too damn complex. So I
streamlined it, uploaded it, took a day trip over to their
headquarters in Chicago and showed it to them. All with this
attitude that they should be glad I did what I did for them.
And they loved it. Asked me to do the same for another
company they owned – which I agreed to do but only at twice
my fee. Which – to my surprise — they agreed to.
Apparently, even though people bitch and moan about
arrogant assholes, those are the ones they most trust to do the
work – so long as the work gets done and done well.
What's also funny is, on the trip to Chicago, I took
my camera. I never take it on day jaunts, not with airport
security like it is. You see, it's this old Pentax 35mm SLR
film camera, and I have a case full of lenses to use with it.
Despite my background in digital everything, I can't stand the
sight of images originating on bits instead of film – and I can
tell the difference, trust me. Besides, I love the feel of that
Pentax in my hand. Have fun using the manual lever to
forward the film. Think the little "click" it makes is joyous.
It's always turned out photographs so precisely, so perfectly, I
couldn't imagine using anything else. So I kept it in top
condition, believe me.
My return flight wasn't due to leave till seven, so
once I was done with Wendahl, I took a stroll down State
Street and snapped pictures of every attractive man I saw –

and wow, did I see a lot of them.

I don't know what it is about Chicago, but it turns out some gorgeous guys. Irish. Italian. Polish. Even black guys with their preponderance of sloe-eyed beauty and café-au-lait skin get my sharp attention in that town. In New York, despite having what I feel is the same basic sociological makeup, the men felt more attitudinal than necessary. And in LA, they just seemed too self-involved. San Francisco is way too cliquish and anti-whatever-you-like for my taste while Miami was just HOT, and not in a steamy way. But in Chicago, the guys just seem – I dunno – easy with themselves in a manner I find brutally erotic.

Like this one beastie I caught striding out of a department store – brown close-cropped hair, dark eyes with lashes an inch thick, a squarish face sliced in thirds by thick eyebrows at the top and a sweet smile at the bottom of a nose that was just plain pert, hints of freckles under tanned skin. I saw him by accident as I was aiming to shoot a gorgeous Romanesque cop standing just down the street, and never gave the cop another thought. My critter had a solid compact body, broad shoulders and trim hips, all packaged in a tailored suit that accentuated his form. He wore an overcoat, but Lake Michigan's icy bluster kept whipping it away from his body to reveal a perfect ass atop damn near perfect legs. He was shorter than me – maybe five-nine – but that was just as perfect. I snapped my lens onto him faster than you can say, "Look." Fortunately, it was a zoom so I could follow him without moving. Ran off a full roll as he jaunted down to a crosswalk, scampered across the street and slipped into an office tower.

Through the lens, I saw him go to the second tier of elevators. As he waited, I shifted lenses to a monster telephoto, caught my last shot of him entering the elevator, alone, then used it to watch the LED beside the elevator doors till I saw that it stopped at floor 38 and started down, again.

Suddenly I felt a Panther roar in my chest, and the need to hunt filled my heart. I focused in on that set of elevators and, without thinking, I jay-walked across the street, aiming straight for that building. Nearly got hit by a taxi, but that only barely registered. I had no clear idea of what I was doing except I needed to get myself up to floor 38. See that guy, up close. Verify that he was as heart-stoppingly beautiful as my camera claimed. In the back of my mind a voice was whispering, "Don't do it; this is dangerous." But I paid it no mind until "Hey! You with the camera! STOP!" tore into my brain.

I froze. And suddenly that Romanesque cop was standing in front of me. Italian features so classic, I got the feeling he could have been a model for Michelangelo as he painted the Sistine Chapel, so many centuries ago. Except he was not happy.

"You tryin' to get killed?"

The blank look I gave him was probably the most honest I'd ever had in my entire life. "What do you mean?" was all I could croak out.

"You walked out in the middle of the street an' almost got knocked down by that cab! Weren't you even watchin' out?"

I jumped back to real-time, then, and said, "Sorry. I ran out of film and – and thought I saw a store over here where I could get more."

Which was a lie. A surprisingly easy one, too. And which would easily be proven as such if he checked my bag, since I had two more rolls of film in it. But he just shook his head.

"Tourist?" I nodded. "Listen up, you want to have a good time? Cross the street at the crosswalk. Lots of these cabs won't stop for ya – 'ceptin' you're out to ride one. Okay?"

I nodded. "Thanks. And I'm sorry."

He winked at me and left. What's funny is, as beautiful as he was I was glad he was walking away. Because what I'd just done spooked me. No, that's too easy a term – it scared the fucking shit out of me.

I'd actually gone into some sort of trance and lost control over my actions to where I'd become this animal sniffing out a meal and working off instinct. If that cop hadn't stopped me, I'd have gone up to the 38th floor, found that guy and...and found some way to get him into bed, whether he wanted to or not. Seeing him had made me not so much horny as just plain – hell, just plain hungry for him. Starving to hold him and caress him and do as I fucking wanted with him. And if that meant I'd have to tie him down to do it, so be it. So be it? So what the holy fucking shit!?

My head began to pound, and I'd left my pills at home. So I found a drug store, downed half a bottle of Advil, grabbed a cab and headed straight for O'Hare, and I stayed in the corner of a bar trying to get drunk till it was time for my plane. And the next day, I called Doug-deux.

He was surprised to hear from me. "Don't you have a regular physician?"

"You're the one who knows what happened. Who ran the tests and – ."

"I can send the results over to – ."

"I just need to know something," I snapped, irritated beyond belief. "Is it normal for somebody like me – who went through this kind of trauma – for me to...to do things without thinking about them?"

"Awake or asleep?"

"Wide awake, in the middle of the day."

"What medication're you on?"

"Oxycontin. Ambien."

"Get off 'em. I'll write up a prescription for Vicodin, for two weeks – after that, it's just Advil or Tylenol, you got me? And for sleep – Tylenol PM, nothing stronger."

I nodded, then realized he couldn't see me and said, "Sure."

"Who's your regular physician?"

"Dr O'Steen, on Campbell."

"Set up an appointment. Have him call me. I'll get your records to him. Have him check you out; make sure everything's healing like it should."

"You think it's the Oxycontin?"

"Could be the Ambien. It can make some people do some weird things. Do you drive much?"

"My car spends more time in the garage than on the street."

"Keep it locked up for another week, just to be safe. If it happens, again, get an MRI. Gotta go. Take care, Alec."

And he was gone. I called O'Steen as he asked then remembered I hadn't contacted Detective Narden. So I did that next. He wasn't in. I left a message then got to work on the new site for Wendahl.

44

Two days later, when I hadn't heard from him, I called, again. He was out. I left a message. He didn't return my call, again.

Now, I know cops are busy. I know they have more cases than they can handle. I know an assault that's ten days old is low on the list of priorities. But at least he could have had the manners to call me back and talk to me about it. If he had, things might have turned out differently. Maybe. But to just ignore me? That'd piss me off before my personality change.

Didn't help that my low-grade headache upgraded to a low-steady throb under the Vicodin. And that Tylenol PM was worthless under these conditions. And that suddenly my once really great ability to concentrate forever would shift into lock-down mode after a couple of hours on the mainframe, and the only thing that would reboot me was uploading an online porn site and wander through their images of big bad boners.

I happened onto this one site that Lonnie must've gone crazy over – some English dudes who "kidnapped, tortured and raped straight guys" while giving them all sort of verbal abuse. Once upon a time, that sort of thing would have creeped me out, especially since almost all of them were uncut. But now? I just watched what they did with dispassion. I knew it wasn't real and couldn't be bothered to bring up that suspension of disbelief to really enjoy it or get outraged by it or even get a serious boner off their humiliation games. I just watched thinking, "Bad acting. Stupid stunts. Why would that be sexy? How could that turn anybody on?" Crap like that.

Anyway, that site linked to another one that was mainly just bondage. Straight guys hog-tied in various stages of dress or undress. Videos of them "struggling" against the ropes and chains. Most of them with the dead eyes I associate with guys who've sold their bodies for a buck, who couldn't even act scared, even while bare-assed and available, even when a couple got felt up and jerked off. It was all just more games and tedious ones, at that.

Till I saw this one guy on there. Short dark hair. Deep black eyes. Shaved his chest but his legs were nice and hairy. Beefy to the point of almost being fat, but not quite.

Not quite. Oh, he was Italian, without question. And in the few nude sessions he did, he'd get a boner as he "struggled" against the ropes. Funny thing is, he'd also grunt and whimper and almost look like he was afraid – and he got through to me. Made Panther's roar become a rumbling purr that could be handled with a few yanks on the knob. I downloaded all of his jpegs and videos.

You see, he reminded me of Woody. And he was in some positions I'd like to have seen Woody in, the little fuck. I mean, I know he wasn't Woody; this guy didn't have the tattoo of a bar code on his hip, his teeth were too irregular and his fat to body weight ratio was probably twice what Woody would have allowed on himself. But he sufficed in my now-warped little brain.

And while it's been years since that prick left me running for the shadows – and even though I thought I'd gotten past it and was moving on – truth is, I still hated and obsessed over that mother-fucking-son-of-a-bitch so fucking much...albeit in the shadows of my mind.

We were together six months, and only the first two weeks were good. No, they were heaven. Everything about me was just right and he treated me like gold.

Except – he didn't, really. He treated me like Gold. Like a piece of jewelry. Like something you wear with a certain outfit or when you're feeling a certain way. And for those weeks, I was his latest bit of bling. I looked sleek. I acted right. I made his friends envious. Especially being a real blond who looked like he'd hung ten for most of his life.

Our first night in his bed was the best, if you could say that with any honesty. We had a nice enough date. Dinner. A movie. Couple drinks at a bar he liked on the wrong side of Lambert Avenue (that's the dividing line between gentrified and slum lord in our fair city). Then back to his place – a normal-looking apartment in a new development, with furniture that looked like it was from a rental house. But we had more wine and listened to music and danced and drifted into the bedroom. And then he tossed me on the bed.

I laughed. Thought it was fun as he fell on top of me. Because what he did next was begin to worship my hair. Run his fingers through my close-cropped do. Caress my eyebrows and eyelashes.

"They're almost clear," he whispered. Which wasn't true, really; my hair *was* a pale yellow, but hardly platinum. And it's grown darker the past few years, to where I'm more sandy, now. But he didn't care. He loved the fact that what I had was consistent...and light...and naturally sparse...and he played with it for an hour.

It was that night that I noticed how perfectly manicured his nails were. They made his strong fingers look like art unto themselves. I felt them drift across my skin. Over my shirt. Pause to tickle at my tits through it. He unbuttoned it slowly. Pulled it apart slowly. Drew his fingernails across my chest slowly. Oh so fucking slowly it was driving me crazy. My dick screamed against my briefs and jeans. My flesh quivered as he whispered his fingers around my rib cage and down my sides, pushing the shirt farther away from my chest. My breath was so soft and quick, I felt like I might faint.

Like I said, I don't have a lot of hair on my body, but his lips and tongue found what there was and took joy in seeing just how lightly they could touch it. And he did that right down to my belly and all over the hint of a treasure trail that fanned out from it.

When he finally began to undo my pants, I was ready to blow if touched wrong. But he yanked them away so suddenly, it startled me. Broke the mood, for a moment – until he nuzzled my crotch, again, sucking at my dick through the fabric of my briefs and running his nails back up my sides.

Then he rose and pulled off his slacks and boxer-briefs and straddled me. Sat right in my lap, leaning back, my crotch caught between the cheeks of his ass. His dick was hard as a rock, too, and he offered it to me without a word.

I rose up and looked at it. Such a nice dick. Big and full and shaped just right. Gorgeous color. I kissed it. Licked it. Thought I'd go as slow with him as he'd gone with me. Hoped he'd let me do to him what he did to me in the gym.

Instead, he slipped it deeper and deeper into my mouth, until I was almost gagging. Held my head there with one hand as the other played with my crotch. I slurped and licked and fondled his balls and did everything I could to give him pleasure, and he shot all over my face after what seemed

47

like just a couple minutes. Then he slipped his hand into my briefs and, with a few strokes, got me to fire my own load into them.

He got up, immediately, wiped himself off with my shirt and headed for the bathroom. He stopped by the door and said, "Got an early client, tomorrow. See you Tuesday." Then he closed the door and I heard the shower start.

I lay there for a few moments, regaining my sense of reality, then rose, cleaned myself as best I could and headed home, feeling vaguely ashamed.

That should have told me what to be ready for.

Tuesday, we went through the same ritual – except this time he worshipped my pubes. Kissed them and caressed them and drove me fucking crazy with need – and then he flipped me over and fucked me. Face down. My head in a pillow. The motion of my dick against the sheets got me off. Then I got tossed out, again. And again. And again.

And it went downhill from there. And even though I'd spent years trying to get it out of my brain, seeing that guy on that site brought back everything, including the thoughts I'd once had of revenge once I'd finally understood what Woody was. Thoughts that had come close to taking me over after my self-loathing shifted to hatred of him, even though I was too nervous and unsure to put them into action.

But in my fantasies? I had Woody bent over a sawhorse, his hands and feet tied to its four legs. Fully clothed in his favorite two-hundred dollar jeans and three-hundred dollar silk shirt. Which I slit off him with a utility knife. Slowly. Feeling every muscle in his legs and arms as the cloth cut away from his skin, leaving him wearing nothing but his silly little jockstrap. He would curse me, viciously, but I'd only laugh and slap his ass. Feel his ass. Rub my dick over his ass and under his scrotum and against his balls. Then I'd fuck him, long and hard, taking my own sweet time as he fought me but could do nothing to stop me. And when I'd cum, I'd fondle and stroke him. Long slow movements up and down. Pinching his tits the whole time. Caressing the hair on his chest and arms and legs. Drive him crazy with need until he couldn't help but explode. Then I'd have Lonnie him bring over some friends who'd like making use of a free ass, especially one as gorgeous as Woody's.

Lonnie had this one black guy he used to be with –
Owen. Chocolate skin. Almond eyes. A smile that looked
like he was getting away with something. I'd never seen him
naked, but his clothes fit well enough so you could tell he was
BUILT. And Lonnie, being the size-queen of all time,
expanded upon Owen's myth by refusing to do anything more
than smile when any of us asked how big he really was. So
Owen would always be the last one to enter into Woody's
sacred portal. It was like an Etienne series of comics come to
life.

Anyway, I jacked off to bondage-guy's image about a
dozen times before I was able to get back to the new Wendahl
site. I finished it fast as I could and uploaded it to their server;
I wasn't ready to face Chicago, again, not just yet. Then I
went down to the police station.

At reception, I asked to see Detective Narden. The
woman barely looked up at me.

"What's it regarding?" she snipped.

"I was assaulted, week before last," I said, already
fighting to keep control of my temper. "I need to make a
statement."

"Third floor, Robbery-Vice," she said, handing me a
visitor's badge. Still not really looking at me.

I took it, attached it to my coat and headed for the
elevator. A guard eyed the badge then lead me into the
elevator, swiped a pass-card over an LED and punched 3.
Then he stepped out. I got the feeling he wanted to sneer at
me, for some reason, but he held it back until the doors closed.

I exited the elevator into an open room filled with
desks behind a counter. A cop sat at the counter, filling out a
form. I went to him.

"Detective Narden, please."

The cop didn't even look at me before he yelled,
"Ray!"

A wary middle-aged man rose from a cluttered desk.
He had the aura of too much cold coffee and not enough
filtered cigarettes. "Yeah?"

"For you," snapped the cop.

Narden motioned me to him. I slipped past the
counter and forced myself to put on my best manners.

"Detective Narden, I'm Alec Presslea. I was assaulted – ."

49

"I know," he said. "That case is closed."

I was startled. "You caught the guys?"

"Couple uniforms caught 'em robbin' somebody else a couple hours later – ."

"No, I wasn't being robbed," I said, trying to keep nice. "They didn't try to take anything – ."

"Got scared off before they could. We got 'em dead to rights, Mr. Preston. No need to worry."

"Presslea. Should I identify them?"

"You get a good look at them?"

"Not really, but I – ."

"Then how can you ID 'em?"

Now I don't know why, exactly, but something about his attitude told me he was handling me like some low-rent-thinks-he's-a-techie rep from Pakistan wanted to handle me – say anything you have to in order to get them off the line. I'd run into it with a number of the telecoms, even after asking for second-tier assistance since I knew the initial guys couldn't handle the problem I was calling about. And they'd do their damndest to insist I let them follow their protocol list before agreeing they couldn't be of assistance and then only because I'd turn into this stubborn asshole out to make their lives miserable. So I decided to run a beta on this skank.

"Well, if they were driving a white Lexus, then – ."

"It's the same guys. But I'll let the DA know that you verified that, and if we need you for anything, we'll get hold of you." Said with a "Now get lost" tone in his voice.

I smiled and left and complained about it that night, to Lonnie and Joseph. Chris was off and his replacement had none of his charm, so all I just sat and drank and commiserated.

"Fuckin' cops!" Lonnie sniped. "You almost get killed and they don't want to bother themselves with it? And I don't recall hearing anything about arrests being made – ."

Fortunately, Joseph was a news junkie. "They caught some black kids robbing a couple in the Gaslight District, that night. One had a baseball bat."

"My guys were white."

"Yeah, one even looked like a surfer."

"But since their truck was black..." Lonnie snipped.

"Shit, I even got part of the license plate."

"He scratched it into the sidewalk," Joseph chuckled.

"I didn't have a pen or paper. Shit."

"He used a rock!" Joseph chuckled. "Call the DA's office, Alec. They're the ones handling the investigation, now. I'm sure they've got someone they think is interesting or have suspects."

Lonnie patted his cheek. "Joseph, honey, one of these years you'll learn – queers don't get the same consideration as normal people. We just get the brush off. I think it's time we formed our own police force and forced some law down the throats of society, as a whole."

"That sounded lewd and crude, Lonnie," I muttered.

"Precisely," he sniped. "And not half as nasty as what I'd do to those little fucks when I found them."

All of a sudden, I felt really depressed. Really down about the probability that I was about to be ignored by the justice system. And felt like there was little I could do about it. I hadn't seen the faces of the guys who jumped me. Hadn't gotten a very good look at the truck. Hadn't been of much help at all in the investigation into my attack. To me, it felt like they singled me out because I was gay. But they hadn't yelled any slurs at me. Just said something like "he's one" before they descended. So why *would* anyone fight to take this case to court? It was shaky, at best.

I thought about it as I walked home, later.

Then I reached the spot where it had happened. Saw hints of blood still stained the area. And saw where Lonnie had scratched the license plat number into the cement – RD4F. And I remembered I'd kicked one of the guys. Hurt his ankle. And he'd been wearing cargo shorts, and his leg was definitely white. As was the slimmer set of legs wearing deck shoes that bounced into the truck. So I decided to contact the DA and let them know this.

I should've waited a while longer. Waited till all the Ambien and Oxycontin was out of my system. Waited till somebody pointed out to me that it's pretty fucking stupid to drink a beer with that crap in you; it messes with your chemical and emotional balance. Maybe things would've turned out different. But I didn't.

And to be perfectly honest, I'm glad.

51

Five

I figured I already knew three things about the guys who attacked me – two of them were white, they were in high school or college (since that's when boys usually bond in their wolf pack thing), and one of them had a black SUV that I think was a Bronco and for which I had a partial license plate. So I decided to share that with the DA assigned to the case. Problem is, when I called, nobody would tell me who that person was. It got the old "Who're you calling? What's this about? Give me the info and I'll pass it along." A blow-off routine if there ever was one – which still pisses me off.

So being the computer maven I am, I found out who it was on my own – one Ms. Lorna Sylvester (swear to God, the first thought that hit my head when I located her was that little yellow bird's nemesis stuttering out "Thuffering Thucotash!"). She was the Deputy District Attorney handling the trial of the black kids accused in the robbery. Only a note or two about my assault in the information attached to the regular files.

Of course, you know where that lead me – straight to the "Restricted Access" files where, and for the first time in my life (I swear!), I hacked into a government database. It was appallingly easy; just find someone with clearance who's dumb enough to use their own name as the password – got four of 'em...and I changed them all, just for fun. But then I thought about it and realized I didn't want anyone to know I'd been there, so changed them back. Hated doing it, but now was not the time to be childish.

At least, that's how I felt till I read the report. Detective Narden's very detailed report. That noted the time, date, place and what happened. Noted my injuries. Said there were two witnesses, one to be considered "less than reliable" (Lonnie, I'm sure). Said no one really knew what was going on; just that they had seen me being attacked and chased the guys off. And had a comment from me that I didn't get a look at them either before or during the attack. Then he noted "another robbery" had been broken up shortly thereafter and the suspects apprehended. One had a baseball bat and the modus operendi was the same, so his conclusion was they were responsible for my attack, as well. Ms. Sylvester's review, posted in another window, was there was insufficient evidence to proceed on my assault.

It all looked great and correct and legal and such...and it was total horse-shit. Nothing about the license plate or the Bronco. Nothing about the kids being white, even though Joseph had gotten a good look at one of them. And it was all written as if Narden had been doing the interviewing when I knew for a fucking fact he hadn't. And it was dated the day after the event, even though I hadn't even met Narden till nearly two weeks later.

So I did a quick cross-reference, found out who the kids' lawyers were and called them all. None of them knew about my attack, and when I let them know what was going on, they grew very thankful. They must have all contacted Ms. Sylvester because she finally called me.

"I just received your information," she told me, oh-so-sweetly. "And I wanted to discuss it with you."

"And isn't it about damn time?" I relied with just as much sugary venom as she offered me.

"Mr. Preston – ."

"Presslea."

"Sorry, Presslea, I have two dozen cases I'm handling, at the moment, ranging from rape to murder. I'm sorry if you believe your attack was being handled in a less than expeditious manner, but one does have to prioritize, at times."

"And letting my attack get blamed on a couple of black kids don't mean nothin', right?"

"Who told you it was?"

"Narden." Give the prick a little tweak.

"He's wrong. No one's blaming them for this. I looked at the evidence, saw it was insufficient to assign blame to any known suspects and left it open to be pursued." The lying bitch.

But I decided to play along. "So they're still looking for those guys? Have you traced the SUV?"

"We tried, but there are no black or dark colored Fords with the numbers in the information given us. It's proven to be a dead end."

So she HAD been given Lonnie's statement. So why wasn't it in the system? Now it looked like playing blond was the smart thing to do.

"Oh. God, Lonnie seemed so sure."

"It was dark. Things happened quickly. People were rushing about screaming. Small wonder he made a mistake. But we are still looking into the attack. And it's still being considered a probable hate crime. My office does not take these sorts of offenses lightly, no matter how rarely they occur. We will pursue the perpetrators will all due vigor, believe me."

Not on your fucking life, will I.

We chatted back and forth a while longer, then she ended the conversation thinking I was a happy little dipshit willing to swallow whatever crap she put in a spoon. But as soon as I got off the phone, I hacked into Vehicle Registration and cross-referenced the partial plate with a description of the SUV and variables on the make. Eleven came up as possible matches.

Eleven.

Hardly what I'd call a dead end.

I eliminated six by cross-referencing insurance claims (one had been totaled and one was in the body shop), citations (one got a speeding ticket halfway up the state within an hour of my attack) and registered home address (anyplace less than five hours drive, which let out three others, for now). I decided to hold off on the two that were registered to females, even though a boyfriend could have been driving the car, which left me with Terrence Hass, Adelano Gomez and Judge Frederic J. Moretti, III.

I gotta tell you which one intrigued me?

Judge Moretti's black Ford Bronco. One of the BIG ones with four-by-four drive. License plate number – "RD4FRD."

Read it aloud and tell me who it reminds you of.
Talk about feeling like an idiot, especially after remembering Freddy's red and grey sneakers and the truck's driver's being the exact same shoes. Shit.

A quick cross reference with parking tickets showed it achieved half a dozen near the state university. A quick hack into the bursar's office showed that, sure enough, Judge Moretti's oldest son, Frederic the Fourth, was enrolled in pre-law. And a quick scan of his very-private, very-exclusive Catholic high school brought me a photo of the dark-haired boy, confirming what I already knew. But the fact that it all was so fuckin' obvious – I was actually insulted.

Fucking Freddy. Gets his rocks off one night; proves he's one of the guys the next. Panther roared at just the thought of the little cunt.

Of course, it being this easy for me to track him down, I knew that Narden and Sylvester knew he'd done it. And decided to keep it quiet. So why would they?

Well, Google up Moretti's name and court and you get all sorts of stories about "Mr. By-The-Book-In-My-Courtroom" who was also despised by public defenders and defense attorneys, in general. Strict interpretation of the law and screw the idea of mercy. Maximum sentencing. The usual right-wing Repugnican activity masked as "hard on crime" but only if you're poor and can't afford a top attorney to manipulate the law as well as he could.

Moretti was once blasted for dismissing a domestic abuse case because both the victim and abuser were female. "If you wish to file assault charges, do so, but the domestic abuse laws are aimed solely at married couples, not people who are not married." He denied having saying it and no one could offer proof to the contrary, so the controversy quickly died out.

There were hints he was considering a run for Senator, but there were also hints he'd fixed a case for someone high up in the local GOP hierarchy – meaning he'd face a nasty fight from the incumbent. Considering the stock he came from, small wonder Freddy liked to beat up queers; he probably thought daddy would think it's only right and proper a thing to do – or knew he would. Or maybe it was just to prove to daddy that he didn't like a man's mouth on his dick

55

or a cock up his ass.

You know, it was at this point that I remembered
Joseph suggesting I hire and attorney to make sure the case
was given priority. And thinking back, I probably should
have. If I'd have my head on straight, I would have – but
something had been broken or cracked open in my psyche and
even thinking about acting in a civilized fashion had shifted
into this alien concept in my scrambled little brain. So once I
understood why nobody wanted to carry this case forward, the
creature deep within growled at the casual injustice of what
was happening.

And Moretti may not have had to say or do a thing
for it to happen; it's just that no cop or DA's gonna piss off
the guy who may be hearing their next case. So Freddy was
gonna walk and I was gonna get pissed on – and this kitty cat
yowled, "No fuckin' way, bitch."

I did one last cross reference – to see if anyone else
had been attacked like me, recently. Turned out a guy was
jumped by five white kids over on Dorral Boulevard (less than
a mile from where mine happened) and was beaten up pretty
badly, as was his brother. The cops called it a robbery, too,
but reading one article I found an interesting tidbit – he'd been
attacked after hugging his brother. Both men were married.
Had kids. No hint of them being gay except for that hug in the
middle of a parking lot, so no connection made to anything
homophobic, at all. Big surprise, that.

Of course, the insta-thought that stirred my growing
anger was, What if they were just mistaken for being gay?
Two guys hugging. Why wouldn't anyone think so? But then
it comes out they're related, so the idea just gets ignored. So
what if the next time the little twerps decided to have some
fun, they decided to be sure it was a real fag they were
bashing. What if that's why Freddy let me suck him off then
split before anything more could happen? Meaning, in my
Vicodin haze, I was targeted.

Only the guys in this story had piled out of a Mustang
convertible.

Still, it made me wonder, so I got Freddy's campus
address and headed over, just to see. Nothing planned or
anything; just working off instinct, again.

When I got there, I realized the address was in North

Campus, meaning Greek World, both male and female. Big houses with weird letters across the front door and manicured lawns and lots of new cars and perfectly beautiful, perfectly well-fed, perfectly coddled entitlement dukes and duchesses everywhere, all sporting the latest in fashion and looking so very Stepford. In college, I'd been both fascinated by them and felt an intense dislike of them all, living their perfect lives and having pathetic little problems to deal with that they insisted were the worst thing to ever happen to anyone...and yet they had such a cool, casual way about them, they were also incredibly sexy.

Like Carson. A guy I was involved with during my sophomore year. Tall. Sleek. Dark-haired (of course). A profile as sharp and precise as an axe, with sloe eyes that seemed to soften it. Built like he was genetically engineered for tennis (and he was on the school's tennis team and did have a slew of trophies in his room). He was an Alpha something or other (I never could get the letters right) as well as an alpha male. Very intense.

And in bed? Holy fucking shit.

We met in a computer lab. I was the de facto techie, even though I was only supposed to be the desk clerk. Part of my work/grant/scholarship/loan packet. He was working on a paper and the system crashed, causing everyone working on it to lose everything they'd been doing for the last hour unless they'd specifically commanded the auto-save to backup more often. He hadn't and was tossing a fit.

I got the system rebooted in under a minute, then started making the rounds to help people who needed it. Most had just been surfing the web and printing out info to use later. Carson had lost everything.

"I can't get it to fuckin' open!" he was screaming. "None of it!"

"Lemme see what I can do," I said, smiling, very much attracted to him. He was wearing a blue tennis shirt with white stripes and a loose pair of white shorts that came to just above his knee and somehow seemed to enhance the shape of his legs. The material was also thin enough to where I could tell he wore briefs, which added to my awareness of the shape of his butt.

Truth is, nothing's ever really lost on a mainframe

57

unless the hardware has been totally destroyed. If you know how to dig in, you can find it and usually retrieve most, if not all, of it. And it took me about six keystrokes to bring his notes back up. Some was scrambled in with ASCII symbols, but you could piece it together well enough to understand it.

As I worked, he squatted beside me and leaned in close to watch, fascinated, his strong, tan, almost hairless arms propped against the desk, his hands wrapped in each other and propping his chin up. I stole a few glances at him – mainly his eyes and their gentle slant, but also at his perfect lips and elegant fingers. He never said a word, unlike the usual types who want to know what you're doing from one second to the next; just shifted his gaze between my hands on the keyboard and the screen. And when his work popped back up, he squeezed my arm and I was sure he was the most beautiful man I'd ever seen.

"Man, thanks! That is so great!"

"I set it up to auto-save every five minutes."

"That's what I got my laptop set up for."

"You've got a laptop?"

"Had. It got ripped off, last week."

"Too bad."

"Aw, it was a piece of shit. But it was all I could afford, so..."

"I know how it goes," I smiled.

Which was bullshit. I'd used my mother's credit card to buy myself the latest in both a tower and laptop and programs before heading for college. And when mom found out, she hit all four walls and the ceiling. My response? "It cost a month's worth of booze for you, lady, and you're not paying a thing for my education, so it's a fair trade." She still tried to stop payment on the cards, but I'd already added myself to them as a co-signer (so she was drunk when she signed the agreement? So what?) and her complaints got dismissed. Took her six months to get over it...or forget about it, which is more likely. And it's not like she couldn't afford it; my grandfather (whom I never met) left her a decent trust fund and set it up so she couldn't mess with it. One more reason dad split – no access to the cash.

Still, being from a smallish town and being uncertain about a lot of other things, I kept low-key about being me. My school wasn't exactly known for its gay-friendliness; in fact, they'd refused to charter some organization because it advocated gay rights, but that was a couple years before me. Now with Carson, I must have all but screamed it in my glances at him because he smiled at me and said, "I'm starved. You wanna grab some dinner?"

Since I was getting off in ten minutes, I nodded.

We ate and talked; what we ate and said was unimportant. Well, to be honest, I don't remember any of it, I was so lost in being with Carson. We wound up in my tiny one room apartment near campus, where I had a couple beers (and yes, I wasn't old enough to have them, but that never stopped nobody, did it?). And we sat at my card table and drank them and halfway through the second one, Carson reached over and kissed me.

It was a rough kiss. He pulled me close and all but slammed his lips against mine and shot his tongue against mine and rubbed his nose and chin against mine and I grabbed him back. It was also my first French kiss but I didn't let the weirdness of it stop me.

I put one hand on his left knee and tickled it up his nearly hairless leg. He shifted forward, giving me better access to his crotch, so I ran my fingers over it. He squeezed his legs together, trapping my hand there, then shifted his hands to my waist and rose, pulling me to my feet. We crushed against each other and groped and fondled and kissed and crushed even tighter together.

To say I was hot for him was to say something like the Mona Lisa is a nice painting or the Sistine Chapel is okay for a church. If we'd kept up like that and done nothing more, I'd have been happy, but it rocketed skyward with him whipping my shirt up over my head and me doing the same to him, then us pressing chest to chest. He was beautifully formed, lean, clean, rock-hard pecs and six-pack abs and no love handles and perky, pointy tits. He pinched at my nipples so I returned the favor.

Then he was yanking at my jeans. Pulled them down over my hips without undoing the belt, pulling my briefs over my butt, with them. I yanked his shorts down, as well. Left his briefs in place. I liked the feel of the cotton against his amazing ass, but he obviously loved the feel of my ass, period;

59

he was kneading it so massively.

My dick was about to explode when he swung me around and we fell onto my narrow bed. He yanked my jeans the rest of the way off, taking my briefs with them, then whipped off his briefs and stood there, for a second, arms extended. The picture he made is seared into my mind, forever – in fact, it reminds me of one of the poses of Da Vinci's Vitruvian Man, even though Carson just wasn't quite as beefy and had a dick on him that belonged in porn, it was so gorgeous.

That's not to say mine's ugly; I'm just average. Like the rest of me. But Carson didn't seem to care.

He straddled my hips, his dick pointed straight at my lips. I raised up and kissed it. Slipped my lips over its head. Cupped his ass in my hands and pulled him closer, so I could take him all. I may have been unsure of myself, in many ways, but I knew how to give head; I'd had practice enough in high school (since girls just didn't do that for boys, in my corner of the world). And I worked him good.

After a minute, Carson shifted around and we got into a sixty-nine position. He wasn't as good at it as me, but I didn't care. He was too fucking right and perfect in every other way for me to give a damn.

Before we came, Carson pulled back and focused on my ass. I'd only been fucked once, before, but by that point he could've gotten me to do anything, I was so pumped up. So I let him take the lead.

He lay me back, put my legs on his shoulders and rubbed his dick and balls against mine.

"Got a condom?" he whispered. I nodded and pulled a packet from under the bed. I only had the one, so I wouldn't be going into him, but that didn't matter. He rubbed himself against me, some more, then said, "Put it on me."

I'd heard it's erotic to do this orally, so I lowered my legs and pulled him closer to me, opened the packet, set it on the head of his dick and used my lips to unroll it. Wasn't easy, to say the least, but he loved it. Then we got back into position and let my spit be the lube and he pushed himself into me, slowly, carefully, elegantly. And then he began to glide in and out and in and out and he fucked me to within an inch of madness, his hands on my hips, his index fingers tickling my pubes, his lips dancing from one tit to the other. I pulled at his tits, too, loving the feel of them in my fingers. Ran my hands down his sides. Wrapped my legs around his waist. Rose up to kiss him and hold him and kiss him and pull him closer to me. God the feel of him working in me – it was like he was the jump drive and I was the USB port (to put it geekily) and everything fit just right. I came first, nearly losing myself in the sensation of it, then I grabbed his ass and manhandled him deeper into me until he also came. He grunted, like a caveman...then collapsed on top of me.

We lay like that for a good five minutes, not moving, not doing anything, just being as one, then he nestled into the area between me and the wall. We spent the night, that way, and I loved him. Wanted to make more love with him. Every night.

Problem is, all he wanted was a fuck-buddy. And I was a good one. But I was also of a mind that we could be more than that, and no way was that gonna happen with Carson. He had a career in tennis all mapped out, and he didn't want to be known as the queer one in the sport (as if he'd be the only one). So after a couple more times together, it stopped. He wound up being seen with a girl around campus and refused to answer my calls or e-mails. I was heart-broken for about three weeks, then got lost in a graphics class whose professor looked a lot like Tyrone Power and let it go.

But being on North Campus and seeing these perfect kids – who hadn't aged a day in ten years – jaunt in and out of their elegant homes brought it all back to me.

Freddy's was a big brick Georgian Style with columns in front and a huge deck in back that overlooked a bean-shaped pool. Trees shaded the place; hedges fenced it in on three sides. With parking for a dozen cars under a long carport, all but two spaces filled. No Mustang, but halfway down the line was Freddy's Bronco.

I parked at a fire hydrant just past it and pretended to be looking at the map I'd Googled up as I eyed the place in my rear view mirror. The sky was bright and beautiful (the first decent day of the year) so the house looked elegant in the sun. It also seemed empty which would make sense, this being the middle of major class periods or maybe mid-terms, since Spring Break was closing in. So staying there was silly. Why not come back later? I don't know. All I do know is, I had no intention of moving just yet – like my Panther had found the watering hole for a group of antelope and was just biding his time till one came up for a drink. And sure enough, one did.

A guy who had the looks of a Quarterback – big smile, sandy hair, bright eyes, tall and buff and cocky as shit – limped out the front door, a walking boot on his foot. His good foot had a flip-flop sandal on it. And he wore shorts, like one of my guys had. And his calves were both hairy and nicely formed and the exact twin of my memory of that guy.

And I all but exploded in my jeans. Seriously, I got hard as a rock, seeing this tall, tanned, sports god of a college brat limping down the sidewalk and across the street and onto a path leading to the main campus. My breathing grew almost still. I felt a growl in my chest. My muscles tensed like I was about ready to spring.

I had a screwdriver in the glove compartment – a Philips. I took it out. Hid it as best I could. Then followed him.

He cut between two buildings and headed for the Quad. I watched his beautiful ass move in a smooth rocking motion as he strolled along. Watched the material of his shorts whisper around solid thighs. Even hobbled like he was, he still had a sexy walk. What made it even more-so was his T-shirt fit his torso nicely and showed off strong broad shoulders tapering down to a waist that was neither tiny nor thick but that was just right. His neck was clean and two-tone around the base of his hairline, indicating a recent chop-job. The epitome of American youth, strolling along without a care in the world.

He greeted some students. Seemed like a popular guy. Of course, no one paid any attention to me; I looked like I could still be in college – or Grad School, anyway – and I was too focused on Quarterback to even pretend I noticed them.

We entered a building. I waited till no one was around then jumped him. Used the screwdriver to keep him quiet. Forced him into a vacant room. Slung him face down across a desk. Yanked his pants down and rammed myself into him before he could figure out what I was doing. He cried out. I slammed his face against the desk and jabbed the Philips into his skin and snarled, "Shut up or I'll cut open your carotid artery." He still struggled a little, but I still was able to grind into him deeper and deeper and yank on his dick till it was hard and force him to cum as I shot inside him and – .

"Hey!"

I jolted. I was in my car, and couldn't figure out how I'd gotten back there. The map was crumpled in my hand and quarterback was just visible between some buildings, walking away as if nothing had happened.

"You can't park here!"

I looked around to see campus security striding up to me. Without even a thought, I held up my map and asked, "Do you know where McNulty is?"

"Oh. Lost?"

"Totally." Again, being blond was advantageous.

"It's on the other side of campus, crosses Grover."

"I knew I should've turned left. Thanks."

I set the map on the passenger seat, put my car into gear and drove away, seeming to be the calmest, most innocent person there ever was. I saw the cop shake his head and return to his little electric go-cart. Then I turned onto Grover and headed for McNulty but pulled into the first parking lot I saw and stopped in a slot and opened the car door and vomited.

I was shaking like a nine-point-nine earthquake. You see, when I'd cum in my daydream, I'd cum in my pants. Without even touching myself. I could feel the wet warmth of it. Still feel the lingering sensation of it. And all twenty minutes of the chase and rape had happened while my hands still held the map and I watched him cross the street.

That I could get so lost in thought it would affect my body scared the fucking shit out of me. But what scared me more was – and this is bad part...this is the part where I should have gone straight to a head doctor – I'd enjoyed it. Loved it. Glorified in it, despite it being just a daydream. And what was worse? I wanted to do it in reality and had honestly told myself, "You should. Show the little fuck – hell, all the little fucks – what it feels like to be victimized."

To say I was now, officially, a total psycho was to

put it mildly – I was now dangerous as hell. And somewhere, deep down inside, I didn't fucking care.

Six

So...now that I had two suspicious characters sharing the same space, I felt it time to learn about the rest. See if any of them might have been part of the attack.

The first thing I did was find out who else was living where, there. This local had sixty-one members, thirty-two of whom lived in the house, full-time. Even if this were a six-bedroom place, that was an awful lot of male energy packed together, so I dug into the city's planning commission's archives and located thirty-year-old plans for renovating the house into a twelve bedroom palace – six upstairs, two downstairs and four in an expansion under the deck in back. Plus each one had its own bathroom – except for two of the upstairs bedrooms; they were at the end of a hall and fairly small with a bath between them, so I figured them for singles. The carport was added eighteen years ago and included three more rooms and two baths at the end of it (and seemed done on the cheap); the pool came with the original house. Since the new rooms were the largest, I figured they were home to three or four guys, each; underclassmen away from home for the first time, most likely, which was still an overload of testosterone living in close quarters.

And the thought of it gave Panther a rumble.

I took another drive past the place, the next day, snapping a number of pictures as surreptitiously as I could, then drove around to the street behind them to see what the chances were of my sneaking some shots of the back yard. I was in luck; the house catty-corner to theirs was for lease, and the ill-kempt condition of the front yard and a couple of broken windows indicated it had been for some time. I noted the number of the agent then slipped into the back yard to see what I could see.

The two yards connected at mine's upper right corner in a spot were the cyclone fence had separated, offering a narrow passageway through some shrubbery into their back yard. I peeked through and got some good shots of everything and was about to back out when a Mustang convertible drove up and parked under the carport. Behind the wheel was a guy who looked so classically Italian, my first thought was, "Must be Mafia." He had that Roman nose and strong chin that are so stereotypical of the northern type, and when he hopped out of the car, he revealed a stocky, well-fed I-A body that just verged on being fat but somehow didn't make it all the way and instead gave off the feel of a statue made from polished marble. His skin was olive-tanned and his legs – he was wearing silky shorts – were the perfect compliment to his body, with a layer of dark hair everywhere to emphasize his perfection. I snapped off a dozen shots of him before I ran out of film.

As he got to the back door, someone popped his head out of an upstairs window and sniped, "Back already?"

It was Freddy.

Mafia flipped him off and continued inside, laughing. I made a mental note that Freddy was in the back left corner bedroom, then I slipped away to develop my pictures and commit my notes to paper.

Once I had the photos and blueprints lined up, I went digging into the school's records to put names to the building and maybe to specific rooms. And listen, I don't care how many barriers or firewalls get put up, if somebody wants to know something from somebody about you and have any idea of what they're doing, they can do it. And I did.

Sixty-one young men; that's a bit above the average number for a Greek house. All of them were aiming for business, pre-law or pre-med, with two political science majors mixed in. Most were from the mid-west, though some were from England, Brazil, Israel and Canada. Of the ones residing in the house, itself, fourteen were underclassmen; the rest were juniors. Apparently all the seniors had condos-by-daddy to crash in.

Unfortunately, the school did not see fit to scan in photographs to go with the names – they probably had hard copies on file in some office, somewhere – but I wasn't all that desperate to see what the cretins looked like. I had their names, ranks, serial numbers and enough family info to do an in-depth profile on them, if I chose.

Next came setting up surveillance. I called the real estate agent and leased the house on the street behind them for a year, using my long-dead grandfather's company for all the pertinent information (since I knew how to hide it in their administration system so it would look legit). Then I slipped into their accounting files and added the management company to "authorized" payees, meaning soon as a bill for the rent came in, they'd automatically send out a check and would probably never wonder what it was for.

On the tour of the place, I made special note of the fact that a back room upstairs had a window through which I could see all of their back yard and into their bedrooms. The agent kept yammering on about "fixing this and replacing that" till I told her I preferred to bring in my own people. When she left, it was with the understanding nothing was to be done to the interior but the exterior was to be completely overhauled. I gave them a week to do it...and they did it. Must have been happy to get the place rented out.

I spent that night up in that back room, using my telephoto lens to watch boys run in and out of the frat house, happy, pissed, healthy, active, totally unaware of life, snapping a few photos of the hot ones as I went.

Mafia was with them, all over the place, and he seemed to be a pretty cool guy. He watched a football game with some. Made a massive sandwich, which he gulped down with two beers while talking with some others. Was on the phone twice with someone who was making him rather upset. Spent some time at his computer – his was the single room in the back right corner of the house. Had a chat with Freddy, when he came home from somewhere, which was joined by a lean-muscled, dark-eyed, sun-bleached, long-haired blond who looked like the epitome of a California surfer-dude.

Of course, that caught my attention. He wore a sleeveless shirt and board shorts, with deck shoes on his feet. No socks. Which I seemed to recall was exactly the same as one of my attackers.

Then another guy drove up in a Beemer and blasted

inside. He sported a soccer kit, was dirty as hell and amazingly sexy for it, with short brown hair, a body straight out of a French Rugby Calendar, legs that didn't quit and the perfect bubble butt, in every way. He grabbed a bottle of something from the fridge, yelled at a couple of guys, jumped up the back stairs, slammed into Mafia's room to greet him, Freddy and Surfer and stormed through the door to the bathroom. Obviously, this was someone who'd never heard of the word "quiet." The door stayed open and Surfer appeared to be talking to him, then he popped out of the bathroom, completely naked. Showed off a set of pecs that were hairless, solid and full and sat beautifully on a six-pack that lead to a semi-shaved patch of pubes and a really swingin' dick. And his tan line? Holeee fuckin' shit, it was just plain exquisite. In fact, the whole moment was so porno, I froze and only got three good shots off before he bounced back into the bathroom, his white-as-marble ass the perfect fit to his beauty. Apparently, he was in the other single room.

What brought me back to earth was when he popped back into the room, still naked...and holding a baseball bat. He swung it, laughing. And Freddy laughed with him. Surfer watched, almost with disdain, it seemed, but Mafia rolled his eyes and said something. So Soccer began swinging his dick at him.

When Quarterback joined them, I felt a rumble behind my heart and a snarl of warning in my mind. "This would fall under the heading of, Way too easy! Be careful, here! Be very careful! Make sure you're after the right guys." And since I didn't want to hurt anyone who'd not been part of my attack, for once I listened to it. Made myself back away from the window (after snapping some more of Soccer swinging both his bats and waggling his ass) and, the next day, dug into when Quarterback hurt his foot.

His name was Jayson Rinaldi (another Italian?!), second year of his business degree but really there for the school's football team. He'd already been scouted by a couple of NFL teams but the Google on him was that he was only good, not great, not yet. He'd probably wind up second-string quarterback and not the big dog, depending on where he came up in the draft. He claimed he'd "twisted his ankle during a pickup basketball game," according to the infirmary records, but he'd come limping into the emergency room an hour after I'd been jumped.

I dug into Jayson's history, a bit more. No trouble that I could find. Not even any drinking violations (yes, I hacked the sheriff's department's system). Parents seemed like nice decent people – father an executive with a local business, mother chief of staff at a local hospital, a sister and a brother, both well into their professions. Seems Jayson came along when the folks were passed forty. And they were Catholic. On committees that were Catholic. Knights of Columbus, even (which I'd never heard of, before). All of them. I found all sorts of articles about them from the one section of the paper I never read – the Religion section. Which lead me to something interesting.

Judge Moretti's family attended the same church. And Jayson went to the same school as Freddy. Plus six years ago, a priest there had suddenly been "reassigned" to a parish in Arizona, which turned out to really be a place for priests with "adjustment problems" to go (I read child molester, here). The circumstances were very deliberately vague, but I did recall Freddy mentioning on his college application that he'd been part of his school's basketball squad. And that priest had coached both the football and basketball teams.

Fuckin' shit. Suddenly Freddy and Jayson were more than a little fascinating. And I began to wonder how I could use that against them.

Now you'd think, if I were still as cool and calm as I've often portrayed myself, that I'd see just how out of control I was getting to be. But all I saw it as was me investigating the crime perpetrated against me in place of the police. Learning more about my assailants. Gathering the evidence necessary to put them in jail, where their pretty little asses would be properly punished by multiple sorts of men over a length of time, thus keeping my lily-white hands clean and pure of their torture while my imagination relished every moment.

Yeah, right.

The truth is, deep in the expanding darkness of my brain I wanted a pound of flesh from each of my attackers. I wanted to be directly involved in bringing them down. I can see that, now. I just kept it wrapped in shadows so I wouldn't have to confront the idea that I was out to do harm to others. What kind of harm was still formulating in my head, since I was still in research mode, but I was beginning to catch glimmers of potential plans and none of them would be pretty or fun – for them.

First I aimed to find out if Freddy and Jayson were linked in any other ways to any of the other suspects. That didn't even begin to pan out.

Soccer was from Chicago. Of course. Cameron Sanderson, nice and white-bread in his AF sexiness. Dad was the office manager of an accounting firm and mom was the stay-at-home kind who also did volunteer work for various charities, none of them religious. He had a sister still in high school, a GPA of 4.1 and a list a mile long of sports related activities. He was here on a sports scholarship, and I found he'd played on the school's football team in his first two years as well as soccer and baseball. No connection to Freddy and company till they'd rushed the fraternity, last year. His Beemer carried some speeding tickets, and I found he'd been arrested for underage drinking a couple of times in high school...and got into a near riot in a park, last year, where everybody swore out charges against everybody else that were then dropped.

I vaguely remembered hearing about it from Joseph so looked it up on the newspaper's website, and it was really just a shouting match between a "number of college youths" and members of an extended Latino family. The Latinos said the college boys were drunk and cursing around their kids while the boys said they weren't, and things had degenerated into a couple of fistfights that ended when a cop car appeared. The DA's office decided it would be too hard to try the cases so everyone walked away...whether they wanted to or not, it looked like. Reading the final report on the county's website, Cameron appeared to be one of the loudest and most obnoxious, not that it was any surprise from what little I'd seen of him.

And this is something I've never really understood. I mean, I sort of get how Freddy might wind up like he did, with a father like that and the family he's got around him, and maybe Jayson was influenced by him. But a guy like Cameron, who has every advantage there is, why he would

70

choose to act like a budding member of Aryan Nation and stir up as much trouble as he could in his obnoxiously entitled way made no sense. Because I never did find anything that made mom or dad or sis or any member of the family come across as racist scum. They were registered Democrats. So how could he come out of a family that appeared to be so nice and normal? The only answer I found was, he was being that way just because he could. And I began to hate him.

Mafia wasn't even Italian; he was a Persian from Beverly Hills and the Mustang was a gift for school. Full name – Reza Shayan Deghati. Why he'd come here was a mystery, since there are two brilliant business schools in the area – though his passel of brothers and sisters might have something to do with it; get away for some peace and quiet. Dad was in "The Biz" and mom headed an organization that was fighting to bring Democracy to Iran, which was bullshit. Iran has elections and all the trappings of Democracy, already; they just didn't elect the people her group thought they ought to elect. And considering how the US elected a criminal idiot to the presidency twice in a row, we had no place to lecture them on the appropriate sorts of people to put into office. What gave their real intent away was, Mafia and all his brothers were given the same name as the Shah with different middle names. Royalists. It figured.

Surfer's name was Mika Anibal, from Rio de Janeiro. His father was in the diplomatic corps and set up at the Consulate in Miami, according to his last notation. But I checked with them and daddy was no longer listed on their roster. Hmm. Probably just a lazy attitude to keeping the school up to date on the pater's whereabouts. He was an only child, looked like, and his mother was dead. Killed in a plane crash in the Amazon, a few years back. That gave me pause. Maybe he was acting out some psychological pain, but still I found it hard to imagine that a kid with his sophisticated background would succumb to homophobia, not when he hails from a city infamous for its free-wheeling sexuality. Plus he reminded me a little bit of Carson, so I wanted to know more before I lumped him in with the others.

So I set up a couple of digital video cameras to record the frat house 24/7 with a direct feed to a powerhouse mainframe. And I made sure I went by twice a day to download the files so it could keep going. Then I researched into closed circuit TV systems and found a beautiful one for retail that offered high-end lenses that could pan and zoom, gave off a super high-resolution image with minimal light and were motion activated. With a few adjustments they could do a wireless feed into a hard drive if located within a certain radius. Meaning I'd decided to find some way into the house and plant the system there.

So what's a little breaking and entering when it comes to justice?

Except I wasn't thinking about what my next step would be; I was just doing it like it'd already been planned. That I'd decided to install those cameras without consciously thinking about it didn't even begin to faze me. I just got ready to do it and figured the opportunity would present itself.

Of course, it did. Spring Break, which was always in the back of my feverish little brain. The boys began vanishing as mid-terms got done, zipping off to catch what fun and snatch what snatch they could. By the time Friday rolled around, only a dozen were left in the place, including my five.

Which didn't make sense. Soccer and Surfer – I mean, Cameron and Mika were done with all classes, according to their schedules, but they still hung around with Freddy, Reza and Jayson, as if waiting for something. I figured they were all going to the same place, together.

But then came Thursday night.

I was in the lease downloading what had been recorded, so far. By this point, three more frat boys were gone and the place was all but empty. My five met in Freddy's room – a room he shared with Jayson (*very* interesting) – for a conference. Cameron brought his baseball bat, Mika his disdain and Reza his cool. After a few moments of animated chatting and guzzling of imported beer, they piled downstairs and into Cameron's Beemer and screamed off into the night, baseball bat still in hand.

Of course, I knew what they were going to do. Had an idea the second I saw the bat. I considered following them but it might have messed with my unconscious plans. So I thought calling the cops, but that would reveal my spying to people who were on their side. So I called Lonnie.

"Haven't heard from you in a while – ," he started,

72

but I cut him off.

"Lonnie, I know who went after me, and I think they're out for another attack."

"Call the cops."

"And have them do what?"

"Right." He thought for a moment then said, "Call the bars."

"I only know the one Chris is at," I said.

"I'll call the rest. Warn them. And you remember Owen? He was talking about getting people together and having patrols. This may be what gets us moving. What're we watching for?"

"Five white college boys in a silver Beemer. I'll call Chris."

"Okay, Alec...wait – how did you find this out?"

"Tell you another time." And I ended the call, then I called Chris.

He was less receptive than Lonnie. "You sure about this?"

"Not really." I figured it was better to play it cagey with him. "But better safe than sorry, you know."

"I'll pass the word along," he said. "Are you all right?"

"Fine."

"You sure? You sound – I dunno – kind of tense."

His concern jolted me. Here it was, weeks since I'd last been in to see him, and he knew my voice better than I did.

"It...it hasn't been easy, lately," I made myself say.

"Come in tomorrow night. Beer's on the house. Let's talk. I feel bad about what happened. How it happened."

"Chris, I – ."

"Stop it. Come in, tomorrow night. We'll talk."

"Okay." And I ended the call. And waited to lose control. Which I should have, almost immediately.

Seriously, a guy I was crushing on, big-time, and whom I'd insulted, had just offered an olive branch. Had offered to let me unload on him. Had let me know I was forgiven for the crude crack I'd made so many centuries ago. Normally, this slams right to my core. And in the past I'd have been weeping with relief. But this time? Nothing. I just sat there in the back room, holding my cell phone, waiting to feel human, again, and nothing came.

I looked out the window. Noticed it was snowing. Gentle flurries that wouldn't be around for long but still a whispering vision of normality. So pure and light. Once upon a time seeing this would have elevated my mood, even if I already *was* in a good one. But again, nothing happened.

It was here – right at that particular moment – that I finally understood certain senses and thoughts and feelings had been excised from my soul. And it felt good and right and proper and empowering, because what was gone was my notion of right and wrong.

I know that sounds like I'd become some amoral sociopathic freak, and it was nothing like that. I'd just been relieved of an *imposed* sense of right and wrong. Like the conventional wisdom that if you're queer there's something damaged about you, even if you honestly believe you're fine and it's just idiots who see you as wrong. That notion – it reflects against your concept of self worth and makes you forever defensive, and you have to acknowledge there are people out in the world who are good and decent and loving who will still consider you a mistake and not some natural part of existence. Which has an effect, whether you want to admit it or not...unless you reach the stage where the opinion of others truly means absolutely nothing.

And that's where I was. Suddenly, being gay was no more my one identifier than being blond or having pale skin or a dick instead of a vagina. It was just one more detail in my life, and the first inkling of this new attitude had sprung forth the day I returned home after the hospital, and I could now see with stunning clarity just how ashamed I'd been of my sexuality. Even after coming out and declaring to the world, "I am who I am," and daring anyone to contradict me, subconsciously I'd still felt that I was not as whole as others. That I had to fight to be taken on my own terms. Now I was just another guy and I didn't just believe it, I knew it like you know you need air to breathe and water to drink and the sky is blue and grass is green...and if you couldn't accept that, the problem was yours, not mine.

What I was doing here, right now, hacking into

databases and spying on my boys without lawful approval, needed zero justification. The legal aspect – or illegal, if you prefer – was a concept that had been imposed upon me by hypocrites who had used the law to hide their transgressions and allow them to continue their evil, so it carried zero validity in my newly aligned brain. The need for justification had become a childish idea backed by prejudice, fear and hate, and this realization expanded from the simple idea that Chris would talk to me.

Four weeks ago I'd have done back-flips if he'd made the offer. Now? All I could think was, "Honestly, I'd rather fuck you." I knew if I did go meet him, that's what I would say. And if he didn't want to, I'd find a way to get to him, anyway, and there would be nothing wrong with it. And this time, the thought didn't bring out the horror that I'd felt in Chicago, because that horror had stemmed from the remnants of the right and wrong imposed upon me by others. Now? Now it would be interesting to see what happened when I did meet him.

I went downstairs and into the back yard. Let the snow tingle against my skin. I wasn't wearing a coat, just a shirt and slacks, but I wasn't cold. I wandered over to the corner of the fence and slipped through and just sat there under the shrubs, watching the house. I could see two of the last boys jaunting around, one in the kitchen and the other in his room under the deck. Nice enough looking but not worth prison, as Lonnie once said. But I still rumbled, deep within. Wondered if I could get both of them at the same time. I'd have to do a little bound and gagged, but once control was made we could have us a competition; lay 'em side by side, jack them off, and the first one to cum gets a pass on being fucked. I smiled at the thought. After all, the one in the kitchen had a trim form and a sweetness to him that would be lovely to possess. And as they left the building for a buddy-on-buddy adventure, I filed the thought away as something to consider for later.

Understand – my new reality wasn't just connected to my dick. It extended to every fiber of my being. I was fantastic in the script-writing (for computers) world, as I'd proven a number of times. But instead of limiting myself to small companies and careful clients, I now wanted to expand

75

to the big dogs. Offer counter-hacking measures. Help those who wished to hide things from others hide things from others, and I didn't care who the others were. In my business world, I was ready to do the stalking.

And what was even better was, I no longer thought Woody was the best looking man I'd ever seen, in any way, form or fashion. He'd become meaningless except as an example of what you could get away with if you were asshole enough, and this diminishment of him let me see the bondage guy I'd once compared him to, not so favorably, was just as good-looking. Amazing what a slap up side the head will do to one's sense of denial. Now I could forget him and become the only asshole in my life.

God, I felt so *real*. So alive and honest and pure, for the first time in my life. My mother was nothing. My father was nothing. My existence was finally my own, again. And here I was, sitting in the gentle snow, watching the world whisper around me as if to say, "Nice of you to join in," and I was loving it. So this was what true joy felt like.

That's when the Beemer returned. I didn't move. Just watched it zoom into its spot and the five pile out, hyper and shaken up about something. I could hear their chatter but their words blended so tightly together, I couldn't make out what they were talking about...until something caught my eye. I had to shift over a bit to see it – but the windshield of the Beemer was totally smashed. And I finally realized Cameron's baseball bat was also missing. I slapped a hand over my mouth to keep my explosion of joy silent.

The little fuckers had gotten more than they bargained for, looked like.

They stormed up to Freddy's and Jayson's room, talking more softly. The cameras were recording, so I stayed where I was and watched them slowly calm down and talk in normal ways. Cameron kept checking himself in the mirror and Reza did nothing more than shake his head, over and over and over. I began to wonder if they'd hit someone with the car, but the Beemer's front end showed no damage, so I doubted it.

Then my cell phone vibrated. It was Lonnie, and I knew without question – they'd been brutally stopped and now were terrified they'd be arrested, and Lonnie wanted to give me the good news and find out more about how I'd known. I let it go to message.

I looked up at Freddy. He seemed to be telling them not to worry, that his father was a judge and would protect them. In fact, he did most of the talking from that point on, and the others listened to him and settled down. Finally, Cameron and Reza went to their rooms and Mika went downstairs to the one he shared with three other guys...none of whom were still there. Crisis over; everything's cool.

Now I was feeling the cold.

I slipped back up to the attic and pulled on my coat...and noticed Freddy and Jayson were seated on a bed, talking. Jayson was still upset, and Freddy's hand was on his thigh. Massaging it. Inching up it. And Jayson seemed not to notice.

I zeroed one camera in on them as much as I could. It caught Freddy's other hand slipping across Jayson's back, rubbing it. Jayson leaned in to Freddy, as if for comfort. Freddy's hand finally found Jayson's crotch and groped it, gently. He guided Jayson back on the bed then reached over and turned off the light.

Holy shit, they were homophobic lovers.

Man, my gaydar'd never even gotten a ping off Jayson. I wasn't sure if that meant he was straight and being used or so deep in the closet he was invisible. Whichever it was, using my Pentax and super zoom, I was able to make out all Freddy was doing was giving him a hand job. And Jayson was returning the favor.

Oh, this was choice. No wonder Jayson couldn't be a great quarterback. He was too busy hiding the fact that he's into tight ends. This was perfection! I spied on them till completion.

I was packing away my Pentax when the two guys from earlier came home, a bit tipsy. One yelled and Mika came out of his room, just in a towel, hair dripping wet. He looked beautiful in it – trim well-proportioned body, dash of dark hair on his chest and up from his pubes, good strong shoulders and arms; he actually made me look forward to making him part of my revenge (now that I knew he was definitely involved). He talked to them, for a moment, then shoved them off to their rooms, went to the back door and did

77

something on the wall – like he was inputting something. I could see his reflection in the refrigerator's black door.

Well – looked like the frat house had security. And I wondered how I'd missed that. I pulled out my laptop and scanned through the pictures of the house but could find nothing to indicate it. So I pulled out my super-zoom and zeroed in on the fridge and saw the reflection of a keypad. I smiled.

This was neither glitch nor problem. It meant the frat house asses would be completely mine once I had the code, because the little twerps would think it's completely safe. And for somebody like me, getting that code is easy. So I smirked and actually whispered, "Enjoy Spring Break, boys. When you get back, it's party time."

And I stood there and watched them all go innocently off to bed as I jacked myself into one of the best orgasms ever.

Seven

The first thing I did was stop calling my boys by their names. It made things too friendly. From now on, they were back to Mafia, Soccer, Surfer and Quarterback.

The second thing was order the DSTV cameras. They weren't cheap, so once again grandad's company was useful. I had them overnighted to my lease, five boxes of the latest in "gotcha" technology with enough cameras to cover the four bedrooms, bathrooms and a few around the place for fun and contemplation and see if my thoughts about the sweet kitchen boy had reason to be considered.

Third was to get the access code to the security system. It was harder than I thought; they had a top rated company protecting their collective asses...so it took me half a day. But it was worth it. Nobody would expect me to be able to waltz in whenever I chose.

Fourth, I called Lonnie to it over with. He was beside himself.

"Honey, it was just like you said! Five of the little bastards in a silver BMW, one with a baseball bat!"

"Where'd they hit?"

"Nowhere. It looked like they were just cruising around, looking for someone. Joseph spotted them, first."

"He was there?"

"He's helping Owen set up safety patrols. He saw the little pricks driving towards the Holiday Club so called the bouncer – he had the guy's number, somehow, can you imagine?"

Knowing Joseph, yes. If you're setting up your own security, bouncers are the best lookouts for trouble and Joseph would figure that out. But I wasn't going to say that to Lonnie. "So nobody got hurt?"

"None of us. But Joseph and Owen caught up and started yelling at them and the kid in the passenger seat raised the bat, so Holiday's bouncer grabbed it away, punched the driver and smashed the windshield with it. My God, they got whiter than white, and did they lay rubber!"

He was nearly dying with laughter.

"Did you get their license plate number?"

"Joseph did and called the cops. They said they'd look into it."

"They won't."

"Of course not, the fuckers. But you said you know who they are – ."

"I'm still looking into it, Lonnie," I said. "I want to be sure before – ."

"Alec, how sure do you need to be?!" I didn't answer him, but one thing Lonnie was not was stupid. "You're – you aren't planning something, are you?"

"I gotta go."

"Alec, don't be an idiot. If you do something to those little shits, you'll be the one in jail, not them!"

"We'll talk later." And I ended the call. Lonnie tried to call me back, but I let it go to message. Now I'd have to keep my profile under his radar. Not good, but considering I'd kept the fuckers from hurting somebody else, it was worth it and fit perfectly into this new attitude I was building, that anything I did was right and proper.

What's funny is, my new attitude got me another job – this time working up the layout and gameplay for a video game. The guys I met with – the epitome of grungy geekiness – had the concept basically scripted out, but they weren't versed in specification-writing or playfield design except in the most rudimentary of ways, and they'd added some implementation details which made no sense but that they really wanted. Seems that's what had pissed off their previous video game designer and now they had to pay up for the privilege of realizing their next dream world. They gulped when I gave them my quote, but I also showed them what I could do and we worked it out to where I'd own a third of the piece, from first dollar, on top of half my rate – which I'd doubled from my previous rate and told them it was half what I usually charged. They'd jumped on it.

Anyway, the cameras weren't scheduled for delivery till Monday, so I spent the weekend setting up the game and ignoring the phone and door. Then segregated out some bits and spent Monday at the lease, working while checking out the frat joint.

It was a ghost house. Not one boy showed his little body during the day. By the time I had the DSTV stuff delivered and spread out and checked and ready to go, it was dark. Time for a reconnoiter.

I slipped into the back yard and casually strolled up to the rear door. Through a window, I could see the alarm's keypad reflected in the fridge; its light still showed steady red. The locks on the door were basic, and I'd noticed one young man who often came in drunk kept a spare key hidden someplace near the bottom of the door. I found a hole at the base of the molding and there it was. I unlocked the door, input the security code – and kept the key to make a copy. Now had my run of the place.

The kitchen was bigger than it seemed from outside and the fridge was packed with beer, water and sodas along with piles of what looked like party food. I wondered if they were planning a bash when they got back. If so, that might prove fun. I headed upstairs via the steps from the kitchen.

I slipped into Freddy's room, first, and dug into both chest of drawers. Seems Quarterback likes boxer-briefs while Freddy's a tighty-whities kind of guy; I took a pair of each. There was nothing else really worth noting; Freddy had very little of his own stuff in the room, aside from clothing, textbooks and supplies, and a computer that he used mainly to surf for porn (yes, I hacked it, and he was big on seeing guys getting blow jobs from girls, though I bet if I'd taken the time to dig deeper I'd have found something else). I was mainly looking for a shirt that would match the navy cotton strip I'd wound up with after my attack. Nothing in this room.

Quarterback had brought some of his trophies with him along with a picture of him and his family, and it was a pleasant portrait, the kind where everybody's dressed nice and posed and happy and content. He had a laptop that he'd obviously used just for school, a Speedo hidden under a pile of

81

shorts (I'd love to see him in this) and a stack of girlie magazines under his bed – camouflage, I supposed. Plus his side of the room was cleaner than Freddy's. A neat freak on top of everything else. Wonder how he'll be after I'm done with him?

Soccer's room was next, and it was sloppy. Dirty clothes piled in a closet (which I refused to dig through), shoes tossed about, bed unmade, a soccer ball resting on the keypad to his computer. I slapped it off; it was just plain dumb to do that. Books were piled all over and he had a lacrosse stick jammed into the closet. A small-screen TV and DVD player were in "pause" so I set them to play and watched some of the junkiest straight porn ever – a woman with tits the size of Texas getting fucked by a flabby younger man as she dildoed her own ass. Gross. He had a couple dozen that seemed to be along the same super-boob lines. He also had a picture of a pretty girl on his desk, and his calendar showed one date circled with "BD, Michelle!!" written in the middle of it. She looked sweet. In his desk drawers were a pile of papers, including one that noted he was due for an evaluation by someone named Dr. Jerrol, who turned out to be a psychiatrist. Soccer was apparently in need of mental re-adjustment, which might explain his part in my attack and his attitudes, in general...and maybe the fact that the only undies he wore were boxers.

I passed through the semi-clean bathroom to Mafia's quarters, and his were well kept. Clothes neat in the closet. Drawers filled with folded briefs and socks and T-shirts, nothing navy. Jewelry in a box atop the dresser. Letters from the folks and family slipped into file folders, with momma constantly worried he's not eating, and photos of his brothers and sisters and their respective others (my boy was the best looking, though one high school lad brought a purr from my inner Panther; maybe in a couple years...). Even his bank info and bills were neat, as was his computer.

Then I found a letter written in a girlish hand from someone named Ella telling him she was tired of being his at-home girl and wanted to break it off. His e-mails showed a lot of back and forth with her, and she'd agreed to meet him for spring break in Cabo (but don't tell the respective parents, please) so they could see how things went. He wanted her to come visit him for the party they were throwing on the 24th. She agreed to discuss it.

I also found some pills in a baggie under the printer. I only noticed it because the edge of the baggie was visible. They looked like aspirin but had an "X" on them. I stole one to see if I could track them down.

Something else I noticed was, Mafia had a chain on his door. I went back into Soccer's and Freddy's rooms, but they didn't have one. Made me wonder what he was up to.

Finally, I went down to Surfer's room. It had three beds jammed against various corners with a locker, desk and chest of drawers bordering them. Above the desks were cheap shelves. Surfer had a lot of literature lined up on his by people I'd never heard of – Palinsky, Ngonga, Feldenaur, Chiang and some I couldn't even begin to understand. Nothing in Portuguese, however. Or Spanish. All English. His laptop was on his desk and held nothing but his coursework. His clothes were minimal and had nothing navy. His drawers were all but clear...except for a small locked box in the back of one.

I pulled it out and checked it, carefully. If I worked it right, I saw I could crack the glue and slip the bottom panel out then re-glue it. So I took it back to the house and did. And what a find.

The box was full of letters from his sister. Mostly family stuff, but they showed that Surfer wasn't Brazilian, he was Lebanese. His last name was really Ibrahim and his father was dead. There were references to a brother in an Israeli prison and positive references to Hezbollah while Islamic Jihad was verbally brutalized. Fuckin' shit, was one of my attackers a Muslim terrorist?

No, that did not compute. I mean, it did explain his reserve with the others. His disdain. But for him to do something as dumb as to go gay-bashing with a group of American jackasses? That was *not* the way to keep a low profile. No, there had to be something more going on here.

I scooted back to the lease and went online to learn more about Ibrahim. He was a higher up in Hezbollah whose car had been blown up by what some believed were the Israelis but was probably a rival in Islamic Jihad. And there was a photo of dad, mom, sis and four boys, none of whom looked the least bit like a surfer...but there was no mistaking my boy's smile and eyes, so no question he was not who he claimed to be; he'd just done a great bleach job on his hair.

The thing is, he'd gone with the other guys, Thursday. And that made me sure he was the surfer Joseph noticed and whose legs I saw getting into the Bronco. But why was he in on it? Was it just the Islamic hatred of gays, even though one of the tortures they practice is butt-fucking their prisoners to humiliate them? I learned about that back when I was working up the site for a group in Canada that was trying to sneak gay men out of Iraq. One of the men they'd saved told about being arrested by one of the militias. They'd tied him over a table and spent hours ramming their dicks into him, asking him if he liked being a woman. Apparently the only reason they didn't kill him was his grandfather headed another militia and wanted the honor for himself. He was able to break free while being taken to a car, found his way to a safe house and made it to England, where he was granted asylum after a lot of uproar. He wanted to come to the US but Canada was the closest he could get since America refused to accept more than two Iraqi refugees at a time; looked bad for the war's PR.

I found a return address had been torn from one envelope – to a post office box in Melbourne. I read more of the letters and learned another brother was at a University in Hamburg, so mom, sis and the youngest boy must be in Australia. I wondered if they were in those countries legally.

Of course a Moslem lying about being from Brazil to get into the US would not be cool with the war on terror crowd, and if he'd gotten caught, the glorious Judge Moretti would've been the first one to turn him over. So why was Mika in the middle of this and cozying up to Freddy? Could the little fuck know about him and be using it?

Easy way to find out, sneered this new voice in my head. Ask him, and do it just before you ruin his life. So I shrugged and figured I would. How, was of no concern; the opportunity would present itself.

I spent the rest of the week sneaking into the house and fixing the cameras in places where they could see and not be seen. Two each in Soccer's and Mafia's rooms; two in Mika's – I mean, Surfer's; and four in Freddy's and

Quarterback's. I also put one each in their bathrooms. Then I set one in the kitchen, one in the den and one on the patio, and even though they were hidden in the walls I covered all their red "activated" lights with black tape to be safe.

I installed two relays in the attic, one over Freddy's room and the other over Mafia's. Then I wired everything into one connection and plugged that to a power strip I'd plugged into the power line. Surfer's cameras were on the edge of being too far away, but I set them to max power and lined up the signal to favor his direction. Took me the whole damn week, but when I tested them out, everything worked just right.

What was fun was, in a corner of the attic over Freddy's room, right where I needed to drill for the lens, I found a stash of forty-odd year old "physique" magazines. The kind where beautiful men from the Fifties and Sixties pose naked except for a tiny strip of cloth covering their genitals. They were in a box and in much used condition. Seemed being closeted was a tradition at this house. I took them with me for later perusal.

Finally, I set up a server to capture the relays. Now I was set, and I couldn't wait. I didn't have to, for long.

The boys came back en masse on Sunday, and I used that day to practice my zooming and shifting and recording. I got some elegant images of good-looking guys stripping down and showing off their tan and burn lines and re-enacting the number of times they'd scored with a girl. I got some great shots of Soccer toweling off from a shower and Freddy greeting Quarterback with a hug that was WAY more than a hug in the privacy of their room and Surfer slipping another letter into his box. It looked like I'd repaired it just right and put it back in just the right place. I also got shots of other cuties getting ready for bed in Surfer's room, including the sweet one who would be fun to play games with. In fact, the more I saw of him the more I wanted to have him – especially when I saw his trim body in a pair of designer briefs and realized how lovely his ass and legs were. Totally worthwhile.

Silly things like that filled the week. The cameras did their jobs so well, all I had to do was some minor enhancement to get it all in glorious detail. And I gotta say,

Quarterback had a fan-fuckin'-tastic dick when it was hard. It wasn't so much long as it was thick as a coke can; hell, Freddy couldn't get his hand all the way around it. Oh, and I caught Soccer jacking off in bed, lights full blast. He turned out to be the kind that showed instead of growed, but he was still beautiful. Mafia was in a mood and a half and spent a lot of his time on the phone, probably to Ella. He did some self-help, too, after one call that seemed to end well, but his back was to the camera so all I had was his magnificent ass to watch...which was okay by me, boss.

I spent the rest of my time ducking Lonnie and working on the video game. I wanted it to kick cojones so I put all my pent up frustration into it, and it was coming along. I figured I'd have its numeric properties set by the middle of next month.

I also looked through a few of the physique mags. They were all from the early Sixties and had been looked at, a lot. I figured it was a closet case who was now in his middle sixties and had left the mags behind because he couldn't figure out what else to do with them, which irritated me until I did a quick check of history and learned being gay could get you put in jail back then, even in California. Shit, and I thought Texas and Georgia were the only places like that. I wondered if the guy'd been a member of the frat or if this was from the previous owner – an old man who lived to ninety and left behind a widow and four children. The mags could have belonging to one of his kids, but they'd all had typical middle-class lives and were dead, too, so I guess I'll never know.

Friday a truck rolled up to deliver kegs of beer. I watched the driver carry them in, two-by-two and drop them onto the patio, the boys gathering round like happy puppies ready to be fed. Then came maid service and trimming of yard and food being nuked and boys fighting over the showers and grooming themselves to perfection. Frat boy mating rituals had begun.

So finally it was time to party with these little animals.

Eight

Things really got going about ten, when the third keg was tapped. Freddy was first in line for a refill, as was this perky little girl he kept tight to him. And they did seem like they belonged to each other; the camera in the den snagged a great view of them kissing and feeling each other up. Later that night, his bathroom cam caught her sitting on the toilet and giving him a blow-job – and not a very good one, from the looks of it. No wonder he'd come looking for a fag to do him right, though I had to admit it fit in with his preference in the X-rated stuff. Maybe he was one of those boys who didn't care whose mouth was on his dick so long as he got off.

I also caught Soccer and his girl, Michelle, in his little room. They started off fooling around, but then he pulled her panties down, crouched between her legs and munched some carpet as he whacked off. His jeans were halfway down his hips, his crack just peeking above the top of his boxers, and both served to enhance the roundness of his amazing ass as he beat his meat. I zoomed in on it. Oh yeah – he got me going.

But it was Mafia who exploded the situation. Just after midnight. Ella'd shown up – a pretty Persian girl with a figure meant for belly-dancing – but they had a fight and she left early, and he was in a serious mood. Until he began chatting up this girl who looked like she was fifteen (but who turned out to be a graduate student). She was cute and had what I call a ballerina's body – very lithe and elegant – with long dark hair and a way of watching everyone while not seeming to watch them. I hadn't paid her much attention. Not till Mafia slithered up.

He sat down by her, and his slinky basketball shorts rode up his thighs. I caught my breath and quickly zoomed in on them. The way his fucking beautiful legs curved and flowed in and out of the neon blue nylon made Panther roar. And they did it in such a way that almost convinced me I should go straight over and introduce myself as his gay bashee and fuck him right in the middle of it all for everyone to see, and the hell with the consequences.

Then Mafia hopped up to get Ballerina and himself a beer, snaking through the crowd in his best shuffly-flip-flops manner. No big deal, in and of itself – except the patio cam caught him setting one beer down, pulling something from his pocket and slipping that something into the other one. I pulled out my camera and watched him with my telephoto lens. Caught a little smirk he gave himself. Caught Quarterback come over and talk to him. Why'd I'd ever thought they were both I-A's – I mean, standing next to each other, neatly dressed and behaving like they had manners, it was obvious Mafia had a far more exotic look to him. Almost beautiful in a spoiled-brat-ego-maniacal sort of way.

Mafia'd drunk half of the virgin beer before he headed back to Ballerina. I followed him with my lens. Watched his little shuffle-walk – that walk that made his ass seem to have a life of its own – as I snapped a full roll of film. Of course, he handed her the one that'd been spiked, smiling sweetly and gently and oh-so-solicitously.

Suddenly I remembered the pill I'd taken from his room. On a hunch, I Googled "Roofies" and found a picture of a tablet – and it was a match. I laughed. Knew exactly what was up. Knew exactly where they'd land – at least, where he'd land her.

I looked at my clothes – jeans, sneakers and a T-shirt – ran some water through my hair to spike it up, grabbed a tiny tube of Vaseline (I used it to help wires slide through tight spots), slipped a utility knife in a pocket and sauntered out the back door. I slipped to my passageway, peeked through to make sure the coast was clear and casually joined the party. In moments, I had a beer in hand and was headed for the back door, pretending to already be a bit loaded. Not one of the college brats paid me a bit of attention.

Until I entered the kitchen. Then a blond girl with one of those "I know you want to fuck me, but you'll never get the fucking chance" looks on her face waylaid me.

"Hi. Who you with?" Her voice was, like, SO California, and her face was about as deep as a saucer of milk.

"Tao of Pao," I popped off, trying to maneuver around her.

Zoomed right over her head. "You a senior?"

"Going for a dissertation," I smiled.

"How'd you get your hair so blond?" Meaning her muff was probably the color of India ink.

"Danish."

"Cheese or apple?" And she giggled, thinking she was being hysterically funny.

"Country." Then I scrambled into the den. Jesus H. Christ, no wonder so many straight guys wanted to be with gay men once in a while, if that bitch was any indication of their choices. While she might be irritating now, imagine how much you'd want to kill her after ten years of marriage.

I did a quick reconnoiter. The couch where Ballerina'd been sitting had a new couple there – Freddy and his piece; kissing, fortunately. I scurried by them, keeping as many others between us as possible. I didn't need to worry; Freddy was putting on a show for everyone so they could know how straight the little shit was...and how I wanted to hurt him. But I headed on up the stairs, instead. I ran into Soccer halfway.

"Dude," he said as he danced on down, followed by Michelle. Not even a glimmer of recognition. I had to fight the urge to ask him if he'd flossed after eating.

The hallway was empty, for the moment, so I slipped into Soccer's room. Set the beer on his filthy desk. Opened the door to the bathroom. Carefully crept through and oh-so-quietly checked the door to Mafia's room. It was unlocked. I peeked in, saw the chain was fixed on his hall door, so gently slipped into the room.

Ballerina was half lying on the bed, near the edge. Her legs dangling over the side. Her skirt pulled up and her panties around her knees. Her blouse was pulled up, too. And from this close, she looked even younger. Of course she was unconscious. Good, no witnesses.

Mafia was so busy grunting and grinding and slobbering over her little tits, he hadn't noticed me, so I got a perfect view of his amazing ass. And realized it's more than little fuzzy. But you could still tell how it flowed so beautifully into his tree-trunk legs. And how it pumped and clenched and rolled as he raped her – though I guess it wouldn't really be rape in his pathetic little mind, not if she never remembered it. And I got a fine view of his hairy balls, too. Bouncing and giving him such joy.

Okay, I thought, I'll show you what joy's all about.

I quietly locked the bathroom door. Then I lowered my zipper very slowly. Pulled myself out and lubed my erection with a generous amount of Vaseline. I was throbbing from touching myself. Hell, from being this close to him. From knowing my cameras in this room were catching everything and I was now crossing a line and could never go back if I did this. But the roar was screaming behind my heart that it was Panther's feeding time, so I slipped out the utility knife, snuck up and fell on top of him. Before he could say, "What the fuck?" I had the blade to his throat and my dick between his ass cheeks.

"Shut up," I snarled.

"Man, she said okay, shit, she said – !"

"You say one more fuckin' word and I'll slit your fuckin' throat." My voice was deep and growling. He shut up. I got close to his ear. "You slipped her a Roofie, you little cunt. I saw you. Can prove it. But I don't care. Stay in her, I really don't give a fuck. Stupid cunt deserves it for trusting a little fuck like you. Keep fuckin' her, all you want."

Then I rubbed my hard-on between his cheeks. He jolted.

"What the fuck you doin'!?"

I wrapped my right arm around his neck. Brushed the knife against his cheek.

"I said, you can keep fuckin' her," I snarled. "But you say one more fuckin' thing, you'll be in jail just as fast as I will. And I'll tell everybody in there she was a kid. You'll get beat up and fucked every night of your life, after that. So be smart. Stay quiet."

"What – what you gonna do to me?"

"What the fuck do you think, cunt?"

I slipped into position. He squirmed. Felt the knife.

"No, man – I'm not that way!"

"You fuckin' will be."

I pushed my dick against the back of his balls. Rubbed against his hole. He began to struggle and shake.

"Please – no, please." His voice was beginning to rise.

I put my right hand over his mouth, the knife still in it. "Fine, call for help. Get everybody in here. Get the cops. Go ahead. Do it. Do it or shut the fuck up and take it."

He was breathing fast. Scared. Still squirming but not as much as before. "This is – this is rape."

I chuckled. "Can you rape a rapist when he's raping somebody else?"

Then I used my left hand to find his hole, lined my dick up with it and pushed the head in.

He fought me. Clenched tight. Tried to wriggle away. But I had him, and I buried myself in him. To the hilt. Felt my pubes tickle against the hair on his ass.

He gasped. Cried out in pain. Choked. Dug his hands into the bedspread. Ballerina did not move.

"Keep fuckin' her," I whispered. Then I started to slide in and out, not too far either way. Pushing his dick against her, whether he wanted it or not. I held him tighter. Wrapped my left arm around his left leg. Felt my hand brush her pubes. Found his balls. I rubbed my thumb against them. Moved my right hand under his shirt, still holding the knife, found a tit and tickled it.

He still struggled to push me out, but between my grip on his leg – and the awareness I had a knife and could ruin his life – he couldn't do much. And it was absolutely beautiful.

He started to cry. Kept whispering, "Please – please."

I shifted my hand to fondle his balls. They were tight. I touched the base of his dick. It felt solid. Not raging hard, but not soft, for damn sure. I began to play with it.

I kissed his ear. He jolted it away. I smiled and licked his neck and shoulders, still pumping all the while. Felt his cheeks push against my hips. Felt the hair on his ass soft against my skin. Felt the strength of his legs push against

91

mine. Felt sweat grow in the spots where we merged. Felt my
heart pound like a jackhammer. The sensation of my jeans
rubbing against my hips and ass and legs nearly made me
insane. The heat from his body seemed to encompass me.
Even the smell of his cologne mingled with the junk in his hair
added to my joy. It was beauty. It was elegance defined.

I felt him grow hard, in spite of himself. Felt him
slip in and out of her. I shifted my hand back to his leg and
held him tight, kept flicking my thumb against his balls. He
squirmed and whimpered and choked back sobs.

"It hurts. It hurts."

My answer was a soft deep chuckle that turned into a
growl that segued into grunts as I slipped in and out and in and
out and – and after what seemed like mere seconds, I felt a
familiar surge begin and I began to pump harder. Faster.
Rammed him into her, deeper and deeper. She still did not
react. I shifted my focus to his beautiful neck. Nibbled at his
hair. At his ear. At his skin.

He still clung to the bedspread. Little whimpers
escaped him. Then, just as I was about to let loose, he jolted
and pushed against Ballerina. His ass clenched my dick so
tight, I thought it was going to tear off. And then he came. I
could feel the shuddering sensations in his balls. Feel how his
dick had become full and hard as a rock. And all I could do
was let loose, myself.

Holy fucking shit, it was the best orgasm I'd ever
had. Like this towering wave of joy screaming from my balls
into every square inch of my body – from tits to toes to my
fucking ears! I felt like I was shooting gallons into him.
Filling him with my cum. Over and over and over and I didn't
want it to end. Didn't want to let go. Didn't want to stop
pushing into him. I molded myself against him. Moved only
my hips. Ground myself into him. Pulled tight on his tit. He
groaned in pain; I'd accidentally cut him.

I finally caught up to myself. Still keeping hold of
him, we drifted off Ballerina. Collapsed to the floor, him
between my legs and me still in him, grasping him tight
against me, daring him to pull himself off me. I could feel my
cum trailing out of him and into my pubes, there was so much
of it. And holding him like that, it only seemed right to fondle

his balls and feel how slick his dick was. How hard he still was.

And realize he wasn't wearing a condom, which might prove awkward later but was typical of scum like him.

Anyway, we lay there – and I could barely breathe, it was so overwhelming. I could have stayed like that forever.

He was sobbing, silently. I finally made myself let go and he just rolled onto the floor and curled into a little ball, his face pressed to the carpet. I looked at him. Thought of how easy it would be to slit his throat. But I figured letting him live with the knowledge he'd been raped while raping a girl, and wound up getting off on the whole process, would be a thousand times more punishment.

I stood up. Slipped my dick back into my jeans. Stepped around him and left through the bathroom. I picked up the beer, drank it and was away from the party in the space of maybe three minutes. No one paid me any attention.

I got back to the house and went into my recording room, purring from satisfaction. I saw Mafia was still on the floor, but lying on his back and with his shorts pulled up to his hips. One perfect leg out straight, the other cocked at an angle. His shirt was open and revealed the hair fanning across his elegant chest. He was just staring at the ceiling, his big eyes barely blinking.

Ballerina was just starting to move.

Mafia noticed. It took him a moment, but he finally made himself rise and pull her clothes back in place. All done like he was in a dream – and yet, done in such a way that I knew he'd had practice. In moments she looked like she'd just laid down for a nap. Then Mafia slipped into his bathroom.

That camera showed him pace back and forth, for a moment, then sit on the toilet. He laid his head in his hands. Then he rose. Pulled off his shorts. Looked at a stain on them. Then he pulled off his boxers and examined them. Crushed them both into a ball. Finally, he lifted the toilet seat and sat down. After a moment, he began to rock back and forth. And then began to cry. I'd have felt sorry for him if he hadn't been such a mother-fucking-asshole.

I shifted to the secondary window to review the footage of what I'd just done. From both angles. I watched

93

Mafia lay Ballerina on the bed. Then undress her just a little. Then pull his pants down. Then get started on her. I entered immediately after that. And stood there for almost a minute watching his beautiful ass move. I even caught a glimpse of me entering him and had a magnificent shot of the expression on his face as he realized he was about to get off on being butt-fucked and then when he shot his wad. And when he rolled off me, I could see a tiny puddle of my cum on my jeans, with some still dribbling from my dick. I also noticed that he never looked at me. Never saw who I was. Just half-reacted when I slipped into the bathroom he shared with Soccer. And wondering if I could use that made me hard all over again. So I watched it one more time, and jacked off to it. And it was almost as good.

Now this is when the manifesto began to emerge. I don't know who actually said, "Vengeance is a dish best served cold," but I knew exactly what the person was getting at. And I also knew exactly how limited that idea was. He was talking about cool, clear, carefully planned and executed revenge, which was really nothing more than an exercise in the childish idea of "an eye for an eye" tricked up in adult clothing but without real passion or need or love. Or hate. And it was wrong to belittle such an elegant notion in that way.

No, vengeance was beauty. Was art. It had to be savored. Dreamed about. Desired beyond anything else you might want in the world. It had to expand beyond the petty boundaries of "just getting even" to bring about real, deep, permanent effect. And what would bring the greatest satisfaction to me in my quest? Beating up or sexually assaulting a group of stupid frat boys because they did something society in general basically tells them it's all right to do? Or sending them to prison where they'd learn nothing but how to hate people like me even more? Or would using them to show the world how completely, totally and absolutely against nature *their* notions are — would *that* be better? Show them how wrong it is for anyone in any society to think that fags are different from everyone else and a danger to the world and that beating up on them is a good thing. After all, as everybody knows, queers have no meaning unto themselves and are to be tolerated, at best. And in this

94

country? We're also devil worshipers hoping to turn all good wholesome American boys into cocksuckers. We're out to ruin America. Destroy marriage. Spit in the face of God and Allah and Yahweh and such. And laws against harming us should be ignored. All of this stemming from ideas so deeply ingrained in our beliefs, it would take a revolution to cut them out.

So what if every time we got hit, instead of demanding equal justice and crying about how wrong it was to hurt us (which has been pretty ineffective, as history has shown) we hit back in a way they didn't expect? What if, every time we were demeaned, we did worse to them? Which lead to what if, every time they killed one of us, we killed three of them?

Well, the realist in me said, they'd go nuts and try to kill us all. And I could easily see that becoming the law of the land. Boy kills fag? Slap on wrist. Fag kills boy? Hang the fucker. They already do it in Iran and Iraq and other parts of the world merely for being gay, let alone actually having sex, and there were some calling for it here in the USA. And those they don't kill, send 'em to jail. But what if – what if every time they hurt one of us, we showed them – proved to them – that what they really wanted to do was fuck one of us?

Now I don't mean using the pseudo-psychological idea that guys who beat up on queers are really queer themselves. I'd already seen that with Freddy and his moments with Quarterback. Revealing him to be one of us would only help to limit society's notions about us and do nothing about the box or category that kept us different.

No, it would be better to go after guys who hated even the thought of sex with a man. Whose dicks point straight at pussies (pun intended). Who would never even think that they wanted to be with a man. And prove to them that *they* were the ones denying nature. That *they* were the ones who were wrong. What if we used physiological evidence to prove beyond doubt that nature meant for men to be with men just as they were meant to be with women? That this is how we were built and that pleasure could be achieved just as well up an asshole as in a pussy, and anyone who said different was lying about something that is normal and natural and the true law of physical science.

Meaning, show the world that men were built to be fucked, just like women. That by putting the prostate where it is and making it so important to sexual pleasure, God really *meant* for men to have fun in each other's asses. That "gay-for-pay" was not just an excuse for one guy to have sex with another guy but was an accepted method of boys doing something that was natural to do with boys. And that the only reason gay men were so hated and feared and whined about was because of simple brainwashing put forth by religious fanatics trying to keep us under their control and operating by their pathetic prejudices, and they were, in reality, the ones who were denying God's plan.

What I'd just done to Mafia almost counted. But while I fucked him, he was fucking a girl, so him getting off could be explained away. What I needed was proof that *any* man, no matter how straight he is or thinks he is – any man could enjoy sex with another man. Could get off on it. Could accept it as a part of his existence. I wanted to show them that man on man sex was as natural and wonderful and worthy as male-female sex. I wanted to prove that sexual natures had been politicized by idiots who hated the idea of honest freedom and wanted to keep men from realizing that they could get their rocks off just as nicely with someone like me as with a girl, and without the complications of possible pregnancy. And what better way to have that idea take hold than through pornography? Something all men have at least a passing interest in, and all women seem to loathe...or, at least, used to. After all, there's a whole genre of "gay-for-pay" websites and videos available to cross reference once the idea had been established.

So I decided, without question, my next mission was to have Mafia fuck Soccer, the one other guy in that house that I knew without question was completely straight. By his choice. On video. And have both of them get off on it.

It would be step one in my Porno Manifesto...and I knew exactly how to do it.

Nine

Okay, how WAS I going to get Mafia to choose to fuck Soccer? The answer was easy – lie. Manipulate. Misdirect. Misinform. Make Mafia figure in his warped little brain that it was something he had to do to get his manhood back. He hadn't struck me as the brightest of subjects, so all I had to do was come up with a good enough story for him to want to do it and all would fall together.

And I already had the beginnings of that story.

But first, I needed to know for sure if Mafia had seen me. I don't think he did while I was on him, but maybe he copped a look I couldn't see on the video. So I decided to test it.

But I had to wait. Seems he was so shaken up by being raped, he bolted from the frat house, and I didn't see him, again, till Tuesday night.

Meanwhile, I got a list of his course schedule, put myself in "pause" and got back to work on that video game. For a bit of fun, I threw in a cut scene that had one hero being sodomized by a minotaur-like beast as his method of losing. Made it comical as all get out. Couldn't wait to hear what the geekies thought about it. The rest I kept pretty straightforward (punning, again) with buxom babes doing everything a boy could do and in the flimsiest of costumes. The little nerds would love that part.

But then I wondered if I should include them in my new mission? I gave it a nano-second's thought, but both were too shlubby. Better for intellectual convincing than physical.

Anyway, I'd just finished polishing another bit of script while waiting for the latest download to complete when

I noticed Mafia had returned. He entered his room, tossed a bottle of something on his dresser and flopped on the bed. I zoomed in to see what the bottle was – a prescription. Xanax, maybe. Excellent.

He lay there all night, not moving. And the pose he held – oh my God. He wore an old T-shirt, light-brown jeans and sneakers. His pecs pressed tight against the fabric of the T-shirt, to where you could see his tits. His right arm lay across his eyes. His left hand rested on his belly. One elegant leg hung off the side of the bed; the other was cocked at an angle atop the bed. His crotch seemed full under the jeans. He looked like he was lying there waiting to be taken.

I did a video-capture of the image and printed it out. To actually hold it as well as see it sent shock waves through me. The curve of his thigh as it drifted away from his hip and gently whispered around to his bent knee. The slight gathering of folds of fabric. The tightness of the jeans around his calf as it bulged and then all but shimmered down to his ankle. The over-sized sneakers stopping the flow of the pants leg. And his other thigh, shooting straight from his crotch to the side of the bed then dangling its calf over the side, keeping his foot just off the floor. The rise of his belly, going from merely flat to a glorious drift away from his belt as he brought oxygen into and out of his lungs, giving his hand the air of a ship caught in a great series of waves. His chest looking almost still, in comparison, and so inviting. The shape of his chin adding perfection to slightly opened lips. He was just plain heartbreakingly beautiful.

My gaze returned to his chest. I dreamed of ripping away the shirt to nuzzle the swirls of hair it hid. Licked my lips at the thought of taking his nipples, one after the other, and toying at them with my teeth and sucking on them till he screamed for mercy. I wondered if it was possible to make a man cum just by working on his tits. I'd have to try that, someday.

It's funny – I'd seen him naked, already, from the camera in the bathroom. Seen his body with its layer of near baby-fat. Hell, I'd even fucking fucked him in his perfect ass. And those were some beautiful images in my mind, let me tell you. But this picture of him fully clothed, lying on a bed and lost in pain – it made me want him more than anything else in the world.

Seriously, I was like a hair's breadth away from sneaking back to the house and trying to get him, again. But this time I wanted to suck him dry. I wanted my face in his crotch as my hands pinched his nubs. I wanted to yank his jeans down and tear off his briefs and swallow him whole – dick AND balls – and show him what a real blow-job was. I was almost dizzy from the mere idea of it.

But then Soccer drove up and jaunted inside. He was in his usual nylon shorts and T-shirt with cut-off sleeves, pouring sweat, with his too-fucking-gorgeous legs, arms and sneakers filthy. Looked like practice was over. He blasted in, hit the fridge for a bottle of something and raced up the stairs to grab a shower, all so fast I barely registered him. I switched to his bathroom cam in time to see him strip off, reveal his bubble-butt and jump in the shower.

Then it hit me – the cut-off T-shirt Soccer'd worn was navy cotton. And the places where it was cut were roughly shorn. It could be the same shirt. Wonderful.

So...the spell was broken. Oh, Mafia still looked hot on the bed – and to be honest, I preferred the shape of his ass to Soccer's; it seemed more real – but now I could wait. Plan to get him when he's open to being gotten. Which would come with time (still with the punning; I got to watch that).

So...the next day, once I saw Mafia head off, I strolled over to campus, positioned myself near the quad and waited till his first class ended. I had a satchel of books and wore a pair of goofy drug-store reading glasses. I milled about till I saw him exit the building then headed to intercept him. He was trying hard to look like he's fine, and doing all right – till I "accidentally-deliberately" slammed into him hard enough to knock his backpack to the ground.

"Shit, I'm so sorry, man!" I stammered in my best nervous voice, and to be honest, I was a little scared. If he did recognize me, I'd have to lie like a motherfucker to get out of it...if I could. But I needed to know, so I kept on with, "I'm late for my lab and I didn't see you."

"Fuckin' shit," he snarled. "You nearly fuckin' took my arm off, asshole!"

"I'm sorry! I was running for – !"

"Yeah, yeah, whatever!" He glared at me, grabbed his backpack and headed off. Not even a glimmer. Perfect.

I felt bold, so I chased after him. Why not get things going, right now?

"Hey, wait! I – I've seen you with Cameron Sanderson, right?"

Still walking, he glanced back at me. "Why?"

"Are you and Cam friends?"

"What d'you want?"

"I – I, uh..."

He stopped and gave me a hard glare. "What? Who are you?"

"I – I'm Brad Phelan. Doctoral program for – ."

"What d'you want, Brad?"

"You know him, right?"

"What if I do?"

"Look, can – can I talk to you for a second? Someplace private? About Cam?"

That got his interest. I headed over to a tree-shrouded area. He hesitated then followed me.

"What about him?"

"Look, I – I don't want to get anybody in trouble here," I said, glancing around a lot, giving him the full nervousness works. "But he – uh – I mean, it's probably just a one-time thing – and – and we'd been drinking and – and maybe he got something I said wrong, or something – but – but..."

I let my voice trail off. Looked away from Mafia. Rubbed my eyes. He was hooked.

"What? C'mon, man, what?"

"Shit, I – I'm sorry. I shouldn't of said anything. Forget I said anything, okay? I'm just messed up."

I started to walk away from him. He stopped me, now clearly worried. "Wait-wait-wait-what're you gettin' at?"

"I'm sorry – I can't – I – look, just – just be careful around him, okay? Don't get wasted around him."

Then I ran off.

"Hey, what the fuck you talkin' about?!"

He tried to catch me, but I have longer legs and do my share of running. I quickly lost him, went back to the lease and got back to work on the video game, my Panther purring.

By this point I'd built up a great spine of false leads and vicious traps for the player, seven levels of attainment available, either up or down, set it all in an urban village of hatred and crime that advanced in stages to either heavenly images of beauty and grace or to a hell Dante would be proud of – where avatars were beaten and in chains, especially when they hurt someone innocent – and then capped it off with a bloodied-up, worked-over version of Soccer's picture as the "game over – you're dead" image. Considering this game was supposed to be PG-13, I was either going to have to do a major clean up or tell the geeks to go for a serious NC-17. But at that moment, I didn't care. I was having too much fun.

When Mafia came back to the house, I watched him bounce around like he was lost. Go in the kitchen to stare at the fridge. Nibble on a slice of cold pepperoni pizza. Gulp down a beer. Watch ten minutes of a game on ESPN then sit at his computer for twenty minutes before bolting away from it. None of the other guys paid him much attention beyond the "What's up" stage of greeting...not until Freddy came in from his classes and Mafia heard him in his room. Then he joined Freddy in it for a long talk...what looked like a very serious talk. For the first time, I wished I'd added microphones to the cameras.

I already knew Freddy would be the weak point in my scheme. He did know who I was, and if he saw me, the whole plan would crash like a ten year-old mainframe. Meaning, I had to make sure he never got anywhere near me, again – not till I was ready for him. So I let things simmer in Mafia's brain for more than a week and gave my full attention to Freddy and his sessions with Quarterback.

There were two more of them.

The first one happened that night, once the house was silent and asleep. Freddy snuck out of his bed, pulled off this pair of ratty boxers he slept in and lay beside Quarterback. The guy rolled over to face him, meaning he'd stayed awake; I guess they had some kind of signal. He pulled the blanket away, revealing he was naked and ready. Freddy played with him, a little, even pinching his tits and running his hands over his flat belly. Quarterback responded by caressing Freddy's body and dick. No kissing or lips to body in any way. Then he and Freddy used their hands to get each other off, again. Almost like a business proposition.

Now don't get me wrong – seeing two good-looking young men fondling each other and pulling on each other's dicks can be hot. And it was obvious Freddy'd had more experience at this than his partner. He even liked to play with Quarterback's pubes and balls. Still, watching two guys do nothing more than mutual masturbation gets pretty tedious after you've seen it twice.

But the next time, everything changed. Same routine, but when Freddy slipped into Quarterback's bed, he wouldn't let him turn around. He just whispered something in Quarterback's ear, flipped the blanket off, molded himself to the guy and started fondling him. Then he wrapped his legs around him and pumped against him, from behind. At first, I thought he was fucking him, but Quarterback was too easy about it. Then I saw the head of Freddy's dick pop out from under the guy's balls and realized he was rubbing between his legs. Lonnie told me that's called frottage, and it got a couple of teenaged boys hanged in Iran.

When he came, Freddy squeezed him so tight, he almost choked him. Quarterback didn't get to reciprocate; he just let Freddy finish jerking him off. It had the weird feeling of being another form of rape, like Freddy was forcing him to accept it. I wondered if I should re-evaluate my opinion of Quarterback.

Freddy stayed in Quarterback's bed for an hour, spooning. Running his hands over Quarterback's arm, side and leg. What Freddy couldn't see was, Quarterback wept through the entire thing. I don't mean sobs, just tears streaming down his face. And the way he not only held Freddy's hand once they were both finished but looked at it, it looked like he was falling in love and hated the realization of it.

It was a haunting image. I did a video-capture, polished it through PhotoShop, put it in a store-bought matte and frame and put it on the wall over my desk, at home. Something about it whispered heartbreak to me. All but screamed, "Here's a man deep into hiding his reality just so he could have a career." And I could see a major crack-up coming with this guy. Probably not till after he'd gotten married and had a couple kids and joined up with some team in the NFL, when the rumors started and he couldn't control them, and which would ruin not only his life but his family's. All because we can't have a fag playing football, can we? Just ain't American.

I seem to recall a soccer – excuse me, football player in England was driven to suicide after he was outed. And that country's relatively accepting of gays. We can get married there...but kids still get bullied into killing themselves and bartenders get beaten to death and the religious scum bark the same message of intolerance, just like here, and one of their football coaches swore he'd never have a fag on his team. So maybe it wasn't all that much better.

Anyhow, I finally had an idea of why Quarterback – Jayson was part of Freddy's pack. He'd do anything Freddy wanted him to. Just like I had done with Woody, for a while.

Which I'd done despite knowing he was no longer interested in me.

That sounds masochistic, especially since he treated me so dismissively. But the fact is, I didn't know it – not really – not in my head or even, really, in my heart. I just knew it deep down, like you sense something but can't articulate why you sense it and find reasons to ignore it. My reason for ignoring Woody's assholiness? Sometimes he would touch me.

That's it. Really. There'd be occasions where we were walking along and he'd reach over and brush my hair back in a way that was so tender, my heart would leap. Or he'd rub the back of my neck. Or just bump me in a jokey way, and I'd feel closer to him than anyone I'd ever known, and I include my mother and father in that equation.

I have no memories of my mother not being on her way to being drunk. Maybe she wasn't when I was a baby, but my first mental image of her is pouring a drink at a Christmas gathering, spilling it on me and having a huge fight with my father. No caresses from her. No concern. Nothing. She never said anything mean or destructive; it's just, by the age of ten I realized I was a chore for her. And I don't know why. I may never know, since we barely talk.

My father – he touched me a few times...with a slap or a fist. This was a man with zero tolerance for children and their inability to act like an adult. Not clean my room? Whap! Not eat all my dinner? Smack! Go to a friend's house and not come home on time? Pow! All from the age of five, until one of my teachers caught me with some unusual bruising and called in child protective services and they sent someone to talk to dad. He never touched me, again. At all. From the age of seven. Then he vanished when I was fourteen and I have zero idea of where he is now...and zero need to know.

But with Woody – sometimes there was this tenderness that would pop up out of nowhere and keep me thinking that we were connecting and could be a couple forever and paint over the growing awareness that it was just a mind-fuck. So he makes a date with me and forgets it and goes out with someone else? He just has a lot on his plate. So he ignores my calls and doesn't return my messages unless he needs something? At least he called me instead of some other guy when his car broke down, because he knew I'd drive the two hours it took to pick him up. But he let me have sex with him, after that...well, he had sex with me, in his usual style. But when you're in need of feeling wanted, justifications come easy and automatically.

The game ended on Memorial Day, eight years ago. He was "short on cash" so we used my feeble little credit card to buy him some fresh gym clothes. He had a new client and had to look his best, as if he could look anything less than. I also paid for dinner. Racked the card up to its limit, which wasn't smart; I needed to get a program for a job I was bidding on and now had no way to do so. It almost cost me the job.

But I didn't care. Woody was being especially tender and close and touchy-feely, and I was in heaven. Maybe we could work this out. Become a real couple. Grow old and cranky together. It was something I still dreamed about.

And to be honest, sometimes still did till I was beaten up.

We got back to his place and played around. He showed off his new things, stripping and pulling them on right in front of me and clowning. Revealing his too fucking beautiful chest and abs and legs to me, over and over, making me horny as hell. Even the fact he kept on his black briefs added to the sexiness – and sluttiness – of the moments.

"I feel like I'm backstage at fashion week," I giggled as I watched him change into yet another set of shorts and tight top.

"I was a model," he said as he waggled his ass at me.

"Really?"

"Yeah. Really. What do you think?"

"I'm not surprised. Why'd you stop?"

"It got boring. And I never made all that much coin out of it. I was too meaty for what they wanted, right then."

"Idiots."

"No shit. You're more like the guys they liked, if you had a bit more muscle on you." I laughed. Woody smiled at me. Caressed my cheek. Took hold of my chin and moved my head around as if he was inspecting it. "Yeah, you'd have done good. Cheekbones. Profile. Hair. C'mon, I'll show you. Put some of these things on."

"Woody, those are larges. I'm a medium."

He pulled me to my feet. "They'll fit. C'mon."

I shrugged and started to undo my shirt, but he stopped me and went through his usual little dance – slowly unbuttoning my shirt and gently drawing it away from my chest and down my arms, his fingers touching me just enough to tingle. Then he unbuckled my belt, slipped it off, unbuttoned my pants and slipped them down my hips. He let his fingers pause and encompass my butt then whispered them around to fondle my crotch. Man, I was about ready to pop.

"Patience," he smiled. Then he grabbed a pair of slinky green shorts and offered them to me. "These first."

I pulled them on. I loved the way the material tried to mold itself to my thighs. He fussed around and shifted them to align just right, then he offered me a matching athletic T-shirt. I pulled it on; it fit loose but not too much so. He pulled out a pair of floppy socks and offered them up without a word. I shrugged and pulled them on, then I slipped on a pair of his sneakers. They were a bit too large.

Woody circled me, nodding. "Damn, you look like you're on the high school basketball team."

"Never was."

"Doesn't matter. What counts is the look."

He was behind me. He ran a finger down my spine, causing the material to caress my sides, then circled his arms around me, crushed himself against me and groped my chest. Pinched at my tits. Ground his crotch against my ass. I could barely breathe, I was so ready for him.

"Okay," he said, "it's time."

But instead of slinging me on the bed, he came around to face me, put a finger in the elastic of my shorts and lead me into the living room. There, he sat me on the arm of a chair and said, "What do you think?"

"About what?" I asked...then saw this African-American guy step out of the kitchen. The stocky, solid, ex-marine type, close to forty and balding who was about to go to seed but hadn't quite started. He wore tight jeans and an even tighter T-shirt and had a leather strap around his left wrist.

"Beautiful," he said.

I stood up. "Woody, what's going on?"

"Just want to try something a little different. You, me and Jack, here, having fun."

"I've never done a three-way and – ."

"C'mon, Alec. Jack's a good guy, and he'll treat you good. So dive in, the water's fine."

"I don't even know him – ."

Woody slipped an arm around my waist and dipped his other hand into my briefs to grope me.

"But you know me, and I say he's cool."

Jack joined us. Put his hands on my chest and rubbed his thumbs over my tits, gently. "And I say, you're beautiful."

I started to push his hands away but Woody stopped me. "Alec, go with it. Let it happen. It'll be fan-fuckin'-tastic. Unless you got something against black guys."

"It's not that, it's just – just – ."

Woody started feeling me up from behind as Jack played with my tits. They sandwiched me between them, their hands groping everywhere. Jack's were rougher than Woody's. And hungrier. He didn't just fondle my crotch, he gripped and pulled at it like he wanted to jack me off into my briefs. And his mouth on my tits – even through the fabric it was electrifying. I got hard, no question, which they took to mean, "Yes," even though I kept saying I didn't want to.

106

Jack grabbed my legs as Woody held me under my arms, and they carried me back into the bedroom to lay me on the bed. Jack yanked my shorts and briefs down to my ankles as Woody pulled the T-shirt up to reveal my chest. I struggled a little and said, "Woody, please..." but he shushed me and kissed me, deep, as Jack took my dick in his mouth and began to pump on me.

Holy shit, did that man know how to give head. Sucking and kissing and sliding up and down and, I'd almost swear, wrapping his tongue completely around my dick to add to the strokes. One hand rolled my balls in its fingers, the other flitted from one tit to the next to pinch and fiddle and tickle and caress. In seconds I was lost in the sensations that shot through me.

Then Jack focused his hands on my ass and Woody took over on my tits, his dick out and hard and hovering over my face. I reached up with my tongue and licked it. Made it stiffen, even more. In response, Woody slipped it into my mouth, and I worshiped it.

It seemed like only moments before I was ready to explode. Jack must have sensed it because he pulled back and let go of my legs. Woody pulled back, too. I looked up and realized Jack had stripped off his shirt to reveal just how extremely muscular he was and had pulled his dick out of his jeans to show just how massive it was. Long and thick and hard as a rock and ready to be plunged into me, and he had slipped a condom onto it, all in a matter of seconds. I tried to shift away, but he grabbed my legs and slipped between them, resting them on his shoulders. My shorts and briefs were still at my ankles, sort of binding me in place...and I remembered the first time I was with Woody and what he'd done and I squirmed.

"No, wait – wait – wait..." I choked out. But Jack put a hand over my mouth and smiled.

Woody got behind me and held my arms. Jack lubed himself up with some kind of gel, then he pushed himself into me with one quick movement.

I screamed at the sudden pain. Woody grabbed my chin and sneered, "C'mon, Alec, you've taken bigger dicks."

"No – no, man...please..."

107

But all that did was bring a chuckle from Woody as he sneered at Jack, "He thinks you're bigger than me."

"I am," Jack laughed, then he began to pump away. It hurt. A lot. At first. But then Woody began jerking on my dick and pinching at my tits as Jack fucked me and fucked me and fucked me, and need took over and let it all join together to make me into a mass of sensation, and suddenly I was at the edge and out of control and firing my load all over myself. Then Jack hit against me, hard, as he finished up. A moment later, he and Woody changed positions and Woody fucked me as Jack caressed my chest and belly and dick and balls.

Jack was bigger.

When they were done, I lay on the bed, sticky from my cum and a second ejaculation of Jack's; he beat off onto my face as Woody pulled out and shot all over me, too. I don't know what I was thinking – no. No...my mind was just a blank. No thinking, at all.

I heard them both take a shower, laughing and playing and comparing dicks and asses in the bathroom mirror. When Jack came out, he was naked and looked like a daddy bear. He lay across the bed, face down and kissed me then whispered, "Let's do it, again, some time. Just you and me."

Woody came out a moment later, a towel wrapped around him, and swatted Jack's ass. "What're you trying to pull?"

"Shit, bitch," he laughed as he yanked away Woody's towel and pulled him onto the bed. "I'm gonna fuck you, sometime."

"Bullshit, bitch," Woody chuckled, but I knew from his tone of voice he was sending the guy a warning.

Jack just laughed and dressed, and they went into the living room. Through a crack in the door I saw him hand Woody a pile of cash. In exchange, Woody handed him a videotape. That was when I noticed the closet door was partially open...and a camera was set up, inside, barely visible. They'd recorded everything.

I got up, went into the bathroom, took a shower, dressed and left without saying another word. All Woody said to me was, "Later." And when I got home, I went online and reported my credit card as stolen, changed my phone number and e-mail address and arranged to have the locks to my doors switched out, all without thinking about it in any way, form or fashion.

You see, it's like a switch flicked in my head – suddenly I wanted zero to do with Woody, period. As desperate as I'd been for his touch, the knowledge that he'd used me as his whore and taped it all for a stranger was too big a slap in the face to ignore. But I still longed for him –like a junkie longs for a fix – and I knew if I saw him, again, or talked to him or heard anything from him, I'd have let him use me, again. And again. Cold turkey was the only way to save myself, and I did it.

I know he tried to contact me because the gym forwarded a message from him – "Alec, where u at? Call me. W." My only response was to cancel my membership. And as soon as I could, I moved here, hundreds of miles away from him and his contagion.

So you see, I had an idea of what Quarterback was going through with Freddy, and it made me kind of feel for the guy. I couldn't say he'd landed any blows on me, or even if he'd really tried. Of course, he was there and had done nothing to stop it, so he was still guilty, but his crime was lessened in my eyes.

In fact, it was looking more and more like Freddy, Mafia and Soccer were the main culprits, and my next step was not going to be sweetness, so far as that was concerned.

Ten

I didn't reconnect with Mafia till the following Thursday. I set myself up on a bench between three of his classes so he couldn't help but see me, and just waited for him to remember who I was. He passed by once without even noticing me. The second time he passed me by, I began to wonder if I'd have to "run into him" again. But then he slowed and stopped and looked back at me. I watched him in the reflection of my sunglasses as he hesitated and studied me. Trying to make up his mind, I figured. Then he came over. I ignored him until he spoke.

"Hey, Brad, right?"

I jumped and looked at him. "Yeah, I'm – uh – oh. You. Listen, I don't think you want to – ."

"No, it's cool, man; it's cool. I just want to talk."

"About what?"

"What you told me, the other day." He sat next to me, glancing around. "About Cam – Cameron Sanderson."

"I told you, I think it was just some – some screwed up communication, or something."

"What happened?"

"Why do you want to know?"

He looked away. I fought a smile and looked at him, hard, as if I was studying his face (and his big brown eyes), and I leaned back.

"Did...did something happen with you?" I asked, carefully wary. He didn't answer. I thought I'd dig at him a little, just for fun. "Are you gay?"

"No!" He all but jumped up. "I never, never – I'm not like those people."

"I am." He looked at me, startled. I didn't move. "I thought that's why Cameron...why he...but if you're not..."

"What'd he do? To you?"

I let him wait a long few moments before I sighed and allowed myself to relax. "He raped me." That had an impact, so I went into detail. "A friend of mine had a party at her place. Cameron's dating her roommate and – ."

"Wait – wait, what's her name?"

"Huh? Uh, Michelle." He nodded and seemed to fighting a growing anger. "Anyway, Cameron was there and we got to talking and I told him I'm gay. I don't hide it and he seemed cool about it, but he did ask me if I liked being screwed. I told him it's great; that he should try it, sometime. He laughed and said he might. All joking and stuff, you know. Anyway, I had too much to drink, so after the party was over I crashed on the couch. I woke up about four. Face down. My pants around my knees. And Cameron on top of me. Inside me. I tried to push him off, but he had me pinned down. So I started to yell, but he put this knife to my neck and he told me, 'Shut up. You know you like it. You said you did.' So I let him finish, and he left."

"And you think he did that to me?"

"I dunno," I said. "I just know, I – I went to see a counselor, and when I wondered if I was the only guy this'd happened to, she told me she had two other clients who'd been through the same thing, recently. And I got to worrying. And I saw you and knew you were at the same frat house as him and I – I just wanted to tell you – y'know, be careful. In case he – he gets wasted, again, and...and..."

"Yeah. I got you." He was focused on me, now.

"Y'know, I – I didn't like it. What he did. It hurt. It's not like when you're with someone you care about. It hurt bad. And I'm still messed up about it. There wasn't anything like love to this. It was just about control. Humiliation. Being the dog on top."

Now he wasn't looking at me. Didn't even seem to be paying attention. So I figured, Plant the first seeds of vengeance – and yes, I said it like that in my mind, just to keep from taking it too seriously.

"Sometimes," I whispered, "I think about getting even. Getting back at him. Do the same thing to him that he did to me. Show him what it feels like to be forced to do what you don't want to do."

Mafia heard that. He hesitated. "How would you? Get even?"

"Listen, I don't want – ."

"I won't tell a soul. Promise. I just – ." He looked down. "What did you feel? After he was done? What'd you think about it? Feel about it?"

"Ashamed." I leaned closer. "He has done it to you."

"I – I'm not sayin' one way or the other. I just want to know how you think you can do it. Get even? Turn him in?"

"Would you back me up? Tell the cops he did it to – ?"

"No! Nobody can know...nobody can even think I...I was..."

"Then he'll just get off," I said. "My word against his kind of thing. No, what I'd do is...I'd do it back to him."

Mafia looked at me, unsure. I nodded.

"Yeah, I would," I said. "Problem is, I'd have to knock him out or get him too drunk to fight back or something and tie him down. I'm not strong enough to make him, just by myself. So he could go to the cops and tell them I raped him and they'd believe him, so...there's nothing I *can* do."

Mafia looked away. I could see the gears beginning to click in his head. God, he was taking it in, easy. Maybe he'd already been considering it.

"I know somebody who's got Roofies." he whispered.

"Really?" I asked, on-so-innocently. "But don't you have to get him to take them?"

Mafia nodded. "He drinks this power crap after each soccer practice. Nobody else likes it. Tastes like chemicals."

"You mean you could spike it? Without him knowing?"

"Probably."

"Why?"

"Because – you're right. He did get to me."

"Oh, I'm so sorry. Was it before or after I talked to you the first time?"

112

"Before. At a party we had at the house. He got me alone and – he – I didn't know it was him. I didn't see the guy, but he left through Cam's room."

"That's a pretty good indication."

"Yeah. And I've been thinking about it, since I talked to you. Things he's said and done. Crap he's pulled. And he never talks about screwing Michelle."

"He hasn't. Word is, he's oral on her. And she don't return the favor."

"Figures."

"I hear that guys who're really down about gays are really that way and don't want to admit it."

"You think he is?" I nodded. "So why'd he pick me? I'm not into that."

"My counselor said rape is usually a crime of opportunity. Did he catch you when you couldn't stop him? Like you'd been drinking or something?"

"Yeah. He did. And it's fuckin' with my head."

"Have to talked to somebody?" Like I gave a fuck one way or the other. He shook his head. "You need to take control back from him."

"Show him what it's like."

"If you'd help me, I'd be happy to do it."

"I want to. I want to fuck him like he – ." He couldn't continue.

"But you're straight. Will you be able to get it up?"

"For this? I will if I have to pop Viagra. I want him to feel every inch of what he did to me. The sooner the better."

"Tonight?"

He looked at me, startled. Then nodded. I smiled.

We made our plans over lunch at the refectory, exchanged numbers and agreed to meet at his frat house about nine pm. Soccer was at practice till then and usually took half an hour to finish talking with his teammates and come home. I was surprised at it being done so quickly, but I think Mafia wanted to get it done before his hate began to lessen and he really understood what he was doing.

I met him at just before nine, at the back door, dressed in jeans and a fleece jacket, no shirt. He was wearing a pair of slinky basketball shorts and T-shirt, and he looked gorgeous in them. He snuck me up the back stairs, nodding to the fridge as we passed it.

"It's all set," he whispered. "I spiked the first two bottles, just to be safe."

"Be sure and throw 'em out when you're done."

He nodded, then we slipped down the hall to his room. So far as I could tell, no one else saw me.

Mafia and I waited there for half an hour. Wondering. Worrying – though more on his part than mine.

"What if he doesn't drink it?" he whispered.

"I'll stay in here," I whispered. "You go in first, to see. And if he hasn't, just tell him some chick called for him but said she'd call back. No big deal. Then we'll wait for him to go to sleep...like he did to me."

Mafia nodded and said nothing more. In fact, from that moment on, he seemed completely focused on a spec of dust floating in the light about twelve inches in front of him. I began to wonder if he'd go through with it, so I snuck a few glances at his crotch. Nothing happening there – though I could easily tell he wasn't wearing undies. Other parts of him were busy, though. Fingers twitching. Fists clenching then opening and rubbing each other. Nostrils flaring. Jaw clenching. Muscles flexing. Breath deep and harsh. Nervous. Could go either way.

Me, however – I was primed to pump, my dick was so hard. The thought of taking control of Soccer and seeing just how much effort it would take to get him to get off on it was hitting me right behind the heart and shooting straight into my balls. I almost preferred he not drink the "kool-aid" and us have to wait till he's asleep. The struggle would be exhilarating. In fact, the thought of it made me so hard and so sensitive, I didn't dare move; if I had, I'd have exploded – or I'd have jumped Mafia, again, and fuck the consequences.

This is where I had my first glimmer of a thought that I might just be fucking insane. A normal man should be freaking out at what I was about to do, and would slip into the usual "I'm not like this" mode, but after everything I'd gone through in the last couple months, it was like some sliver of my DNA had shifted from dormant to active and I could honestly see either course of action – raping Soccer with Mafia or just raping Mafia, again – as being a good, solid,

114

sensible one. And the serious, honest-to-God certainty that I could carry either one off was just a given, in my brain.

And I do not know why; I honestly had never pulled this kind of shit before. But somehow I just plain knew that if I turned on Mafia, I'd have him tied down and under control before he could formulate the idea that he should call for help. As for Soccer – hell, that was even less of a question, if he drank the spiked water. And that made my logical side question wonder if I should back out of it – not out of a sense of fear but the vague notion that I was not thinking on a logical plane.

I mean, what the fuck *was* I doing? Aside from committing any number of felonies that could slam me into prison for the rest of my life? And *why* was I doing it? Yeah, I wanted to get even with the fucks who'd fucked me up, but I could do that by raising hell in the press and filing lawsuits left and right. And, yes, there was my manifesto – but hadn't that really already been proven by the gay-for-pay porn stars out there? Wasn't what I was doing just an extreme example of the fact that in the right place and at the right time, anyone is capable of anything?

What's funny is, I still thought of myself as a good guy – a "good guy" who was now guilty of breaking and entering, fraud, identity theft and sexual assault. If I'd been Catholic, I'd never have been able to say enough rosaries to make up for it (Lonnie told me all about it). And if I got caught? Well, I couldn't use an insanity defense; everything I'd done had been with deliberation and careful planning. And sitting here with Mafia, it became blindingly obvious I was probably fucking myself over as much as I was these punks.

I looked Mafia over, again. Focused on the curl of his dick and richness of his balls, barely hidden behind the clingy fabric. Let my eyes follow the flow of his thigh as it filled the shorts and glided from behind the hem to whisper up to his knee. His hair lay soft against his skin and swirled around to flow down his full, elegant calf and pull in tight to emphasize his thick ankle and long elegant foot. I realized his feet were bare and his toes were lean extensions of his entire leg, they looked so right. I was about to reach over to run my fingers along the top of his foot when we heard Soccer's Beemer squeal to a halt and him blast inside in his usual hurricane-like fashion, clump up the stairs and lumber into his room – and the spell was broken.

Mafia looked at me, startled. I looked back with a half-smile. He rubbed his palms together.

"How long does it take?" I whispered.

"Few minutes."

We heard the shower start up. A picture of Soccer standing under the steaming water, rivers coursing down his muscular back and over his bubble-butt and down his gorgeous legs got me going even harder. I could see my hands grabbing his cheeks as I swallowed him, whole. Could feel my fingers massaging his skin. Now I seriously began to wonder if I really could keep from getting carried away and let Mafia do the only fucking.

I snuck another look at Mafia's crotch, and I saw it beginning – his dick just a bit fuller and twitching. He wanted to do this. And now I wanted to let him.

Mafia rose. Pulled at his crotch. Slipped over to the bathroom door. I stood and watched as he opened the door and looked inside. Just past Mafia, I could just see Soccer crouched down in the shower, the water dancing over his back. He was holding his head. He half fell to a kneeling position.

Mafia froze, so I headed in. Pushed right past him.

"Come on," I said, softly, then grabbed Soccer under the arms.

He looked at me, groggy and confused. "What th' fuck – ?"

"Yeah, what the fuck," I shot right back at him. I pulled him to his feet. His legs were wobbly and he nearly dropped to his knees, again. I motioned to Mafia. "Hold him up."

Mafia wrapped his arms around Soccer's chest, shaking his head. "Dude, why'd you do it? Why the fuck – ?"

I shushed him, grabbed a towel and dried Soccer off. Lingered a bit around his magnificent ass and played with his dick and balls a bit more than was necessary. Then we carried him into his room and flopped him on his bed.

He rolled about, trying to get up but unable to control his actions. Watching him made me even harder, the way his arms flexed to no effect and his legs shifted around in their

116

beauty and his dick flopped from one side to the other. I looked at Mafia. He was glaring at Soccer, breathing hard but not moving. His dick was visibly at the in-between stage of soft and ready to go.

Soccer managed to maneuver himself to the head of the bed, but still had no real control. Mafia seemed unable to move.

"You want some help?" I asked.

He shook his head and yanked off his shirt. I pulled my jacket off. Then he grabbed Soccer by the ankles, yanked him to the side of the bed and twisted him onto his stomach.

"What – what's this –?" Soccer could barely mutter the words.

"Payback," Mafia snarled. Then he yanked his shorts down. His dick was harder but not yet ready as he knelt between Soccer's legs.

"Be easier if you used some Vaseline or baby oil," I whispered.

Mafia jerked a nod and stood. He went to the bathroom.

I climbed onto the bed and guided Soccer to beside me. Lay him down next to me. Fondled his dick and balls as I sucked on his tits. He sort of tried to push me away but had no strength.

"No – don't wanna – not me..."

But his dick was getting hard. I could feel it growing. So I whispered in his ear, "Liar," and held him close.

Mafia came back with some baby oil. I'd seen him use it on his skin, when he was tanning. He looked at me, confused.

"Like that?"

"Makes it easy for both of us," I said. "I'll help you."

I slipped both hands around Soccer and grabbed his cheeks. Pulled them open. Mafia dribbled some oil on Soccer's hole and I smeared it on as he lubed himself up. Watching him was the purest definition of erotic, the way he squirted the oil down the length of his shaft then rubbed it smooth, making it hard and ready and worthy of a porno shoot. I all but prayed the cameras were getting a good view

117

of it. Then he lay behind Soccer and I helped the head of his gorgeous dick push up to...and then into Soccer's hole.

Soccer struggled, a little. Whimpered. Tried to roll away. But Mafia and I had too tight a grip on him, and soon Mafia was all the way in and pumping away.

"No...no...don't..." was all Soccer seemed able to say between grunts of pain or discomfort or even pleasure, maybe.

I let Mafia control Soccer's torso as I ran my lips down the trail of his hair to his navel and then down his treasure. My fingers caressed his dick and balls the whole time so when I finally arrived, he was close to being erect. I wrapped my lips around him and got to work taking him the rest of the way.

I have to say, Soccer had a beautiful...fucking beautiful cock. I felt like I was, I dunno, worshiping at a temple, it was so exquisite. The shaft perfectly round. The head perfectly formed. His balls perfectly oval and just loose enough to enjoy. I could have spent hours doing nothing more than sucking on him and licking on him and toying with him and might still do that, just for the hell of it. But what made that moment perfect was Mafia pounding away at his virgin ass.

No ropes. Nothing to make it seem like he's being raped. Just three guys lying on a bed and making a sandwich with one of them. Rather like Woody and Jack had done with me. Of course, I could tell Mafia was having trouble getting to the point where he could get off. He was grunting and pushing too damned hard. So I let my fingers slip between Soccer's legs to play with Mafia's balls. No serious groping, just something extra to help him along as I kept my lip-worship going.

After a few minutes, I could taste that Soccer was getting close. Could feel his head starting to swell. He'd stopped fighting us in any way and was just letting out little groans. But Mafia was still not quite there. So I worked Soccer even harder. Gripped his dick with my free hand and pumped on him like I was a milking machine.

God, it was great. I could almost feel the differences in the veins on his shaft as I ran my tongue over them. And the ridge of his head fit into my lips like they'd been formed at the same time. He tasted pure. Clean. Then a bit salty. Then meaty. He quivered. Jerked back. I could feel him filling up and squirming and hear him gasping and tensing and then he exploded. First in my mouth and then, when I pulled back, halfway across the bed. Over and over. I could feel his ass clench tighter with every ejaculation. I watched them spring from within, beautiful little arcs of white fluid, rich and opaque and oh so lovely to see. His dick bounced as they leapt across the blanket and landed into little pools of sensuality. And when he was done, while his dick was still hard and bouncing about from Mafia's pounding, he kept spurting some here and there, including a couple of shots that landed on my body.

Mafia's movements began to stutter, like he was almost there but couldn't quite hit it. So I grabbed his ass with both hands and kept him pumping. And then I felt him clench up and knew he was letting loose, so rolled away from him with Soccer and let him finish ejaculating onto the bed. I didn't get a good look at him as he did it, but I could tell from how harshly he was gasping, it was a good one.

I did notice he was collapsed on the floor, one arm still clinging to the bed, barely able to catch his breath. I thought about jumping him, again, but Soccer shifted about, trying to get away from me so he became my focus.

I rolled him onto his back, crossways on the bed. Then I took out my dick. It was raging and ready. I gently opened his mouth and slipped it inside. He gagged and tried to roll away, so I straddled him, grabbed his head and slapped my dick all over his face. Then I yanked on it until I was ready to fire – which took less than thirty seconds – pried his mouth open, again, and slipped into it to let loose. I let my first shot of semen slap against the back of his throat then pulled out and let the rest cover his face.

It made me weak, like when I'd fucked Mafia. I saw stars – well, sparkles that seemed like stars – and wound up holding his face against my crotch once I was done shooting. Let my dick rub my cum against his eyes and nose and mouth and cheeks and chin and hair, extending the sensation as long as I could. And the whole time I was doing it, I was watching Mafia.

He just sat by the bed, unmoving, facing three-quarters away from me. Still breathing hard. I could see his left leg, cocked at an angle and elegant from it. His right arm just lay on the bed, beautifully formed but seeming like it was weak. His hand was palm up.

I let go of Soccer, stood up, put my dick back in my pants and went around the bed to Mafia. Squatted before him. He looked at me, confused. I smiled...and gave him a deep, long kiss. He pulled back a hint, but stopped and let me continue. No tongue; that would have spooked him too much. When I ended the kiss, I looked deep into his eyes. Stroked his chin. Moved a strand of hair away from his face. Gave one of his tits a pinch. He gasped, involuntarily. And I smiled.

"Welcome to the club," I whispered. "Now you're a man."

Then I grabbed my hoodie and left. And as I walked down the hall, I decided my next trick would be having Freddy get fucked by the four guys he brought to my bashing.

Eleven

So how was I going to do that, one might ask? Blackmail. Yes, that good old-fashioned American way of making you do something you don't want to do via threats and intimidation (mixed with lies and a healthy serving of misdirection). And I had enough on Soccer, Quarterback, Mafia and Surfer to destroy their young lives if they didn't follow my instructions...once I figured out what those instructions would be.

But first things first. I finished the Beta of the video game and delivered it to the geeks, all prepped for them to ferry it to an animator, then I took them through the first three levels of play. They loved the big-boobed "companions" I'd worked up. They actually giggled like school girls when they got to look down one's "cleavage" and almost, almost see her tits. It was hysterical, but what's crazier is, I started glancing at their crotches to see what effect my work was having, and I was not disappointed, since both little shlubs apparently wore boxers and one looked like he'd been given the gift of endowment in place of beauty. Too bad he needed to gain about twenty pounds to look slim.

Then we hit level four and my first real cut scene – the chunky geek's big buff avatar got to screw a big blond Valkyrie worthy of a big bad Wagnerian opera. I even set it up so he'd get a little buzz on his board when he "came." He jumped up, laughing girlishly, and ran to the bathroom. Talk about a participatory imagination.

The skinny one looked up at me with big-lashed eyes and asked, "Are there more like this?"

"Better," I said, almost smirking.

121

He nodded. "We'd like to finish reviewing the game in private."

I grinned and left.

Later they called, suggested some changes in the tone of two levels and punishments and said that would be perfect. Not a word about the Minotaur raping the avatar. Maybe they hadn't noticed what was happening, though I'd have run every possible outcome if I was going to lay in some top-level graphics, and they seemed just as anal as I'd be, so I could only assume they hadn't been bothered. I got the last payment and a contract guaranteeing me part of the income and that was that. Now I could focus on the boys.

Except that's when Lonnie and Joseph decided to stalk me. They found me at an electronics store as I was buying a micro-digital camera.

"Alec, where the hell have you been?" Lonnie shrieked the moment he saw me. Joseph was close behind.

I jumped and almost ran away. Seriously. But Panther kicked in and I faced him head on.

"I've been busy," I said. "Why?"

"We're worried about you, you little shit. You never come out, anymore. You've closed yourself off from everybody."

"I got a job working up a video game. It's taking all my time and – ."

"Then why're you never home?"

"I am. I'm just not answering the door or my phone."

"You could return your calls."

"I'm busy!"

"Every day of the week? Twenty-four-seven? Chris says you haven't been to the bar since – ."

"Fuck Chris. Fuckin' prick tease. I don't go back there because I'm tired of him playing me." Then I noticed the clerk ringing up my sale had eyes as big as headlights and was glancing between us all. I snarled, "Done yet?" He wasn't.

That's when Joseph finally chimed in. He'd been watching me throughout, and it was starting to spook me.

"Alec, have you seen a doctor?"

"Why?" I snapped. "You think I'm crazy?"

"A physician. Someone to run an MRI or CAT scan. The way you're acting – this isn't you. You need to be examined."

That jolted me, a little. I remembered Doug-deux and what he'd told me to do so long ago, and I'd forgotten my appointment with O'Steen. My headaches had diminished so I'd felt there was no need. But here was sweet gentle Joseph trying to find a reason for me suddenly being this complete asshole and offering me a life-line back to my previous existence. It shifted my whole mood from defiance to weariness.

"Guys, I'm sorry. I've been so lost in this game, it's warped my personality. I – I'm delivering it, tonight. Then things'll be okay. Okay?"

"What kind of game is this?" Lonnie asked.

I went sort of dreamy and whispered, "Extermination. Destruction. Deliverance. Rebirth."

"Not necessarily in that order?" Lonnie tried to quip.

I just smiled. Joseph put a hand on my shoulder.

"Alec, it's just that we care about you and – ."

"Why?" I asked, as I looked at him.

"You've gotten lost in a project, before, but you've never been like this and we're concerned."

"No, why do you care?"

"What?"

"Why do you care? I've never treated you right."

"What do you mean?"

"You're always there for me. For Lonnie. For all of us. And we treat you like shit."

"Hey," Lonnie snapped.

"You treat me fine."

"It's not right. You'd be the perfect partner for somebody – shit, for me – but all we seem to want is guys who look like Chris or Woody or any of those fucks of Freddy's, even when they're assholes who dick us around and – ."

"Those fucks of Freddy's?" Lonnie asked. Oh, shit. "Alec, you said you knew the guys who attacked you. Is that who you're talking about?"

I froze. Couldn't think of a thing to say that would sound reasonable. I focused on signing my credit card receipt. The clerk was ready to leave, he was so shaky...which would

123

have been fun if he wasn't such a chunk. Lonnie got more intense.

"What sort of game are you playing, here?"

The words just sort of drifted out. "Extermination. Destruction. Deliverance. Rebirth."

"Are you talking about bytes or reality?"

"Who can tell, anymore?"

"Alec, please," Joseph whispered. "You're scaring me."

I looked into his big beautiful eyes. So tender and kind. The type of guy who'll always be your best friend, even if you use and abuse him. Who knows right from wrong and cares about it. A sweetheart who goes home alone because he doesn't have what we demand as beauty. Not ugly. Not even plain. Just not like Woody. So sad. So terribly-terribly sad and stupid.

I drew him close and kissed him full on the lips, in the middle of the store with dozens of heterosexual patrons gazing on, shocked. I could just hear the clerk screaming in the back of his brain, "Oh my God, George, next thing you know, the fags'll be fucking in phone accessories!"

When I pulled back, Joseph was looking at me, confused. Lonnie, for the first time in his life, was speechless, which was a joyous thing.

Joseph tried to speak. "...Alec..."

I put a finger to his lips and smiled at Lonnie.

"It's a video game, guys. That's all. Drop by tomorrow. Around six. I'll show you what I've been up to."

The both eyed me like I was a visitor from another planet, and I probably was, at that moment, so I grabbed my camera and got while the gettin' was good.

It was time to finish the game.

I went home. Printed up four invitation cards – one for each of Freddy's buddies. The message was simple – "Meet me at the address below or I'll send you to jail...come alone" – and I set them up for two different times, then I put the address of the lease at the bottom and each went into its own envelope with the boy's name on it. I had a courier service deliver them to the guys in class.

Then I went to the lease, relocated the mainframe to the attic, set up a TV in the back room and connected it to my

124

laptop. Once I saw it was working, I placed a sturdy table before it, hid my three cameras in spots where they'd record to maximum benefit, then hopped downstairs and set up some lights as I kept an eye on the front.

Sure enough, at seven on the dot, Surfer warily strolled up. Even though it was still chilly, he wore nothing but his board shorts, t-shirt and deck shoes. I wondered if he even owned a coat. I opened the door.

"Hi, come on in."

Soccer eyed me warily, as if he almost knew who I was.

"What's this about?" His voice had a musical accent to it that could have been Brazilian but wasn't Latin enough. He showed me his card. I took it, smiling.

"You gotta come in to find out," I replied.

"I don't know you."

"Yes you do. I'm the fag you, Cameron, Reza, Jayson and Freddy beat up a couple months ago."

"I dunno what you talk about, man. I'm leaving."

"If you want. But I'll just call immigration and tell them all about you."

"I have a visa – ."

"For Mika Anibal, not Mikail Ibrahim."

His eyes went wide at that. I stepped back. He hesitated then followed me in. I closed the door. One of the lights was already illuminating the room; it cast a hard shine on half his face and body and warmed the area. I'm sure he appreciated it.

"What do you want?"

"Take off your clothes."

"No." He pulled a knife – a switchblade, to be exact. It flicked open with the cutest little "ssslick." I wondered how I'd missed finding that in his room. "No man touches me."

I sighed with weariness. Seriously. I was not the least bit afraid of him, somehow.

"I don't intend to touch you," I said. "I just want to see you. Strip and stand on that material." I motioned to some black cloth I'd draped from the upstairs landing. Another light was near it.

"No." He moved toward me with the knife.

125

"Mika, I know where your mother, sister and brothers are. That information is set to be forwarded to immigration, and they'll share it with Germany and Australia. I have to keep it from being sent. Now you don't strike me as a stupid guy. Don't put yourself in Freddy's league – though I would like to know how he got you to run around beating up queers with him."

"You are mistaken. I – I have done nothing wrong – ."

I took a deep breath. "Just before Spring Break, you guys went looking for another fag to bash. Instead, Cameron got his windshield shattered and you almost got caught. That *was* dumb, Mika, especially for someone like you. Now take off your clothes."

He began to shake and sat on the bottom step. He looked near tears.

"Please, if you tell about me, my family will be killed."

"I won't say a word – if you do as I ask."

He looked so young and scared, sitting there, his legs lovely in their lean muscular way as they slid into his deck shoes. He was still cold; I could see goose bumps on his arms and his tits were pointy. And Panther was yowling.

"Well?"

He rose. "What will you do with me?"

Fuck you, hit my brain, but what I did was hold up my Pentax. "Keep the knife. I won't get within ten feet of you."

He looked at me. Up close, his face held no disdain or even real fear. Just confusion, and it gave him a nearly angelic beauty, almost like something Caravaggio might paint.

"You want to bring me shame."

"I want you to take off your clothes. And I'm not asking, again."

He hesitated, then closed the knife, held it between his teeth and yanked his shirt over his head. He kicked off his deck shoes, untied the board shorts and they dropped, then he stepped out of them. He was completely naked...and my heart nearly stopped.

I normally don't go for the slim twinkish type, but while he'd been pleasant enough to look at in his usual costume, naked he was fucking elegant. Perfect proportion from his shoulders to his taut pecs to his trim hips to his strong legs, with a dick and balls that were just right for the picture he made, even in the cold. Soft hair flowed up his belly from his crotch, swirled into a tight cord above his navel then fanned back out when it reached his chest. Going down, it whispered around his thighs to dance down his calves. His arms were heartbreaking in their sinewy strength. Not an ounce of fat on him.

I circled him, and from the side he was just as lovely. Same for his back – strong shoulders tapering down to an ass that was smallish but just the right size for him. Hints of hair danced over his cheeks, and they looked joyous. I almost reached over to caress them, but then I remembered his knife. No sense testing him, yet.

"Stand on the cloth." He stepped over to it, knife still in hand, and stood to face me, hands at his sides, legs spaced apart, lips pursed, his eyes never leaving me, almost defiant.

I hit the switch to the second light and it slashed across the material, behind him. Now his body was cut in half by light and shadow, with the shadow side framed by the slash of light on black cloth, adding a soft glow to the edge of his hair and the line of his body. The lights warmed him, so his dick relaxed and his balls began to hang from his scrotum, making them look even lovelier.

"Open the knife," I said.

He did. It gleamed in his right hand. I snapped off five full rolls from dozens of different angles and positions. He did not move.

"You know about my father?" he finally asked. I nodded. "The bomb – it was meant for all of us. We left the day we buried him."

"Smart move. Who's this Anibal guy?"

"His wife knew my mother. He helped us to hide. He is a good man."

"If you're a good boy, he stays out of it."

"I never hit you. Never hit anyone – ."

"I know."

"Then why do you do this – ?"

"You were there. Okay, upstairs." I started up the steps. He didn't move.

127

"What will you do with me?"

"Would you rather I fuck you? Is that what you really want? Are you one of those closet cases who needs to be – ?"

"No! It disgusts me! This is not a man's way."

"Bullshit!" I snarled. "I'm going to show you what a man's way is. I told you I wouldn't touch you and I won't – unless you want me to. Now come up the stairs!"

I cast him a quick motion to follow me. He finally did, grabbing his clothes, en route. I smiled.

"Leave 'em."

He dropped them by the stairs and headed up, passing me. I watched how his legs and ass moved as he climbed. They were like music in their gracefulness.

I lead him into the TV room and hit the space bar on my laptop. Three screens popped up on the big screen – two on top, one below. The upper left one showed me raping Mafia, though you couldn't tell it was me, yet. The upper right one showed Mafia and me raping Soccer, and again I'd edited it so I couldn't be identified. The lower one showed Freddy with Jayson, to which I'd added a couple insertion shots to make it look especially perfect.

Surfer grimaced and turned away.

"These're your buddies," I said. "Taking you out to beat up queers then fucking each other, in celebration. Why'd you go with them?"

He looked at me, brutally confused. "I – I didn't know."

"Maybe the first time, but..."

"They told me to go with them, again, and I thought I must. But I never hit you!"

"You said that. Why do you think they invited you?"

"What do you mean?"

"There's twenty-six other guys they could've taken along. Why'd they ask you?" He fought for an answer. "Want my idea on it? You're a good-looking kid, Mika. Nice body. Cute ass. Maybe Reza or Cameron or Freddy got a thing for you. Not Jayson; looks like he was probably your predecessor. But they figure you're even less into that, so they come up with a way to force you. Take you out. Commit a few felonies. Then one night, Freddy gets you into his room

128

and says, 'Y'know, Mika, I got the bluest balls and my right hand ain't cuttin' it, no more, and you sure got a pretty mouth. So how 'bout you take of me?' And when you tell him to fuck off, he says, 'Do it or I'll throw your fuckin' ass in jail and you'll find out what a fuckin' ass really means'. And the next thing you know, he's shootin' his load down your throat."

That shook him up. Big time. I began to circle him, still smiling. Made a slow, wide arc, but he didn't notice. His eyes were locked on the videos, now. The way his back flowed down to his cheeks and his legs were spread apart made the view so inviting, Panther yowled for joy.

"That's what happened to me," I said. "I was the I-T guy for his father, the Judge. Freddy figured out I was gay and in the closet, so he made me service him. I'd have lost my job if I hadn't done it. Over and over. Then one night I said enough; the next night, you guys beat the shit out of me."

I was standing behind him, now, and he was shivering. The room was warm, so I know it wasn't from the cold. I strolled up to him and gently took the knife away.

"I can see why Freddy'd want you," I whispered. "The way you fit together. And he likes virgins. Jayson was one before Freddy got to him. You know how he does it? I watched him. Shot that video of them. It started like this."

I embraced him, from behind, my arms holding his in place. It took him a moment, but he tensed and tried to move away.

"Wait – you said – ."

I held him tight and fingered his tits as I whispered, "Shh. I won't do anything to you."

But holding him tight, like that – my arms wrapped around his, my fingers touching the hairs on his chest, his trim body molded against mine, my crotch pressed against his ass, my dick hard as a rock, the Panther screaming for its food – without thinking, I reached down and groped him. He jolted and kicked, so I shoved him face-down on the table and crushed against him. He struggled. I still had the switchblade in one hand, so I flicked it open and pressed the point to his throat.

"No – you said – you wouldn't – I didn't hit   I didn't do anything – !"

"You were fucking there," I growled. "Roll over."

129

He hesitated. I dug the knife into his skin. Drew blood.

"ROLL OVER!"

He shifted under me so we were lying face to face. Now he was quaking with fear. I opened my fly and pulled out my dick. It pressed hard against his and Panther roared.

"You're gonna take it, bitch, or I'll cut you. And your family'll get found out and sent back to Lebanon to die."

"Please – no – I didn't..." He fought to maintain control.

"I don't care."

Then I pushed his legs apart with mine, used my free hand to find his hole, pressed the head of my dick against it and shoved it in. He cried out and fought me but his struggles just made me chitter with joy. His whimpers of pain made my heart leap.

I kept the knife at his neck as my other hand groped and fondled and pulled at his dick. He stayed soft for most of the ride, but near the end he began to grow and expand and join in with the animal need in me – and it was so much more than merely carnal, what was happening here. Every nerve in my body was on fire from being in this guy's ass. Every push was like a thousand moments of tingly joy; every pull was like a tide of emotion dragging my heart with it, and they carried me close to madness as I slid in and out and in and out. He grabbed the sides of the table as I pounded away and lost myself in the one focus of drowning his virginity with every ounce of cum that I could muster.

It seemed like mere seconds before I was exploding inside of him over and over and over and...I nearly blacked out from the overwhelming beauty of it. Nearly drowned in the nirvana it wrapped around me. Nearly wept from the warmth of his skin against mine. The tautness of his muscles as I kept flowing in and out and in and out. Nearly cried out with joy at the feel of his dick being that stage where it's almost...almost hard but not quite, and so much the lovelier for it. Everything swum together in this mélange of drunken ecstasy from the orgasm I'd achieved, and I did everything I could to prolong the wonder. It took me several minutes to drift back to earth and look at him...gaze upon his smooth face and dark hair and golden skin.

And I noticed he was crying. Bawling...and it made me want to scream with happiness.

I let myself stay inside him, for a while, just to savor the perfection of it. Then I slowly...slowly pulled myself out, wiped my dick off with my shirt and rubbed his neck. I ran my fingers over his tits. Such pretty pecs he had. Then I slipped my hands down his smooth little belly to his dick and fondled him, some more. He looked pretty, but he was already losing what little erection he'd achieved, so I bent down to caress the head with my lips and tongue.

He gasped and tried to swipe me away, so I grabbed his wrists, held them out to the sides of the table and lay on top of him, crushing my still hard dick against his. I licked at his tears, almost chuckling.

"I met a man from Iraq who had this done to him for a full day and night by a dozen different motherfuckers, and he didn't cry. He knew if they saw his tears it would only get worse. But don't worry. I'm finished."

"What – what're you – ?"

"Stay here, just like this."

"No, I – want to go."

"Then you'll leave naked. First, I want to tell Freddy, thank you."

He looked at me, fighting the tears. "What?!"

"Didn't you notice? That's me in two of those videos. How do you think that happened? To make up for the beating, Freddy set up Mika and Cameron, then he said I could have you before he does."

"Wait – Freddy set this up?"

"How else could I've known what class you were in? So stay there. I'll be right back."

And I left him. I grabbed his clothes, dropped his shirt on the first step, lay his shoes at the top step and left his board shorts by the door to the TV room. Then I put my Pentax in its case, hid it behind the curtain and went out the back. I slipped through my opening to the frat house's yard and strolled up to the back door and knocked.

Now, if my timing was right, the fun was *really* about to start.

Twelve

Several boys were engrossed in a hockey game, but the sweet one heard me and came to the door.

"Yes?"

He looked even nicer, up close – sloe eyes and gentle smile on a smooth yet trim body under a button-down shirt, fitted jeans giving shape to nice legs and the promise of a great crotch. Yes, he would be fun, another time.

I held up a CD-R. "I'm here to see Freddy Moretti. Got some graphs from Friedman economics for him."

Sweetie nodded and yelled, "Moretti! Back door!"

Freddy rounded a corner and saw me and stopped cold. He was in shorts and a loose Tee, flip-flops on his feet, a bottle of beer in hand. Still fuckin' gorgeous. I held up the disk. "Hi, Freddy. Got something for you."

He recovered quickly and said, "Up here." He headed up the back stairs. I followed, casting one last glance at Sweetie as he hopped back to the hockey game. Freddy may have the better legs and ass, but that kid moved like a poem by Whitman. Panther purred.

We got to Freddy's room and he yanked me inside as he snapped, "How'd you find me?!"

Through his window, I saw a shadow move in the corner window of my leased house. If I was right, by now the other boys had found Mika in the TV room, and one had noticed the view of Freddy's quarters. I looked at him, making sure a smile never left my face.

"I happened to be on campus and saw you and followed you here," I smiled. "The CD-R was a ruse."

He looked at me then smirked and said, "So what you want? A repeat?"

"You do have a lovely dick."

"You're fuckin' crazy, dude. My roommate might catch us."

"And he might join us. I've sucked off two guys at once."

"You've been watchin' too much porn."

"Studying it, actually. I'm writing a dissertation on how pornography can be used to further a political agenda. I'm calling it my 'Porno Manifesto.' Care to be part of the study?" And I batted my eyes at him.

He laughed. "That's sick." I just grinned in answer. He actually glanced around the room and out the window, thinking. He finally said, "I dunno. Might be better if I come back to your place, some night."

I got close to him. Put my hand on his crotch. Gently massaged it. He started growing.

"But I'm here now. We could go in the bathroom. That way, if your roomie does show, I can slip out the other door."

"Got it all figured out, huh?"

"Most good sluts do."

"But that stuff you said – about one nighters..."

"Who's looking for a relationship?"

He spread his legs to give me better access to his balls. I tickled them, gently. Rolled them in the white cotton fabric that held them so perfectly. He sighed.

"You do give good head."

"Practice. And I've got something new I'd like to try on you."

He let me pinch a tit. Took in a deep breath. Backed to the bathroom door. I paced him, keeping my hand on his crotch. He was getting bigger by the second.

"Just remember," he said in a husky voice. "No ass."

I smiled and we slipped into the bathroom.

I sat on the toilet and positioned him before me. Ran my hands up and down his elegant legs. Reached up under the shorts almost to his balls. Tickled the hair covering his skin with my fingers. Then I undid his fly and slipped down the zipper and the shorts dropped to his knees. He stood there, dressed in his tighty-whities, his dick pushing against the material.

133

I pulled the briefs down to let his dick fly out.
Freddy was more than ready. I stroked it. Juggled his balls.
Flitted my tongue through his pubes and up his abs. Ran my
lips along the length of his shaft and over the nicely formed
head. He still smelled of peanuts, and I wondered if it was
because of the beer.

"Oh, man – don't tease."

Then I heard someone jumping up the stairs, so I
slipped my mouth over his dick and all the way down. An
instant later, the bathroom door crashed open and Cameron
roared in. Before either of us could say a thing, he punched
Freddy to the ground! Then he slammed my head against the
sink!

"Motherfuckn' faggots! Cocksuckin'
motherfuckers!"

Reza joined him in pummeling me, and this time
their fists were connecting. Constantly. My vision crashed
into a blur and my head began to ring. The last thing I felt
was my nose break. Then I was on the floor and blood was
everywhere and people were screaming and someone was
kicking me and I was laughing.

I woke to find Doug-deux gazing at me, his smirky
eyes looking very worried.

"So, he's back," he said. I tried to speak but he
stopped me. "Your jaw's wired shut. Got a bit broken, as did
your nose, three ribs, your right forearm and your right
collarbone. So you'll be a junked-up soup man for the next
couple months. Hope you like it."

I shrugged. Tried to reach for his gorgeous face, but
couldn't raise my hand. I looked at it and saw I was
handcuffed to the bed. I looked at him, confused.

"This is the security ward of the hospital," he said.
"Seems you're up for sexual assault. On the son of a judge, no
less. And I hear you used a switchblade to force him.
Meaning kidnapping. Who knew how dangerous you were?"

I snorted. He nodded.

"I think it's bullshit, too. But I got no say in the
matter. I'll keep the cops away from you as long as I can.
Give you time to get your wits back. You have a lawyer?"

134

I nodded and motioned for something to write on. A nurse came up with her clipboard and let me write "Winslow in wallet" on it. Left handed. Doug-deux nodded.

"I'll see he's called. Get some rest."

He left and I drifted away.

I kept drifting for two more days before I was able to focus enough to face the police. I would come to and find a pair of uniforms or suits hovering over me, trying to get an admission that I was worse than a child molester. I'd just look at them in my Darvocet haze and Doug-deux would say something like, "Told you so," and shoo them away.

Winslow was corporate law, but he called in a colleague from a law office six floors below his – this short cocky pit-bull of a guy – who was escorted in by Doug-deux during yet another attempted interrogation my second day in the hospital.

"What're you doing?" he snapped at this basketball-player of a detective then looked at me. ""Mr. Presslea, I'm Garrett Udall. Paul Winslow asked me to take on your case. Is that all right?" I nodded, so he went nose to navel with the basketball guy. "My client has nothing to say."

"We need a statement and – ."

"And you'll get one. Now get out."

They snarled and fumed but got. Doug-deux grinned and got with them.

Then Udall turned to me and said, "So, I hear you're scum of the earth." I shrugged in answer. He laughed. "Good. So what's your story?" And we got down to it.

It wasn't easy using my left hand to write with, but I still managed to tell him about being bashed and how I'd tracked Freddy down. I said nothing about what I'd done about it; instead, I told him I'd tried to get the DA's office to go after Freddy, but they'd refused to. Udall nodded.

"I've dealt with Judge Moretti. He's a prick. So what'd you do then?"

I told him I'd been watching the frat house and noticed Freddy and friends leaving with a baseball bat, so I'd called my friends. Then they'd come back with a smashed windshield, and I mentioned Joseph got their license number.

"The same guys who beat the shit out of you in the Moretti kid's bathroom?" I nodded then frowned and held up two fingers. "Two of 'em? And Moretti was the third. Who were the other two?" I shrugged. "Were they there?" I frowned and shook my head, as if not sure.

I don't know why I did that, but I think I had an idea Mika and Jayson *had* been tricked into the first bashing by Freddy and had been coerced into going along on mine. So I felt no need to further their humiliation. In fact, I was actually feeling sorry for Mika and what I'd done to him, so I decided to minimize his involvement.

"Well," Udall smiled, "that gives me something concrete to shove in the DA's face. Shouldn't be a problem finding out if Sanderson's BMW's been worked on, lately. Now tell me, what happened in Moretti's room?"

Something I'd noticed was, not once throughout any of my interrogations or in talking to Udall had anyone mentioned the videos I'd made of Freddy and friends. Or my cameras. Or the mainframe in the lease. Nothing. They were making out like I'd been caught forcing Freddy to let me suck on his dick and that was all. So I decided to play with it.

I told Udall that I'd realized the DA was going to do nothing about the info I'd given them (so what if they pointed out I'd never given them a thing; I'd just say they're lying) so I'd decided to ask him, myself, why he'd done it. I'd used the ruse of a CD-R to get him to talk to me. I also told him about taking Freddy home the night before the attack, and gave him Chris' number at the bar to verify it. Then, I said, one thing lead to another, Freddy'd said he was open to a repeat, we'd gone into the bathroom and then Cameron and Reza had slammed in, struck Freddy and pounced on me.

"He ever tell you why?" Udall asked.

I nodded and told him about the coach/priest who'd been reassigned from Freddy's school. That he'd molested Freddy and I reminded him of the guy. So he had this love/hate thing going about being serviced then thinking he'd been used and flashing back to the initial molestation. All lies, but they wrote out well enough, and Udall liked it.

"This will be fun, especially once the judge hears about it. Make you a bet – all charges dropped within a week."

I smiled, innocently. He smiled back then leaned in close, his lips twisting into a wolf-like grin.

136

"You gave me plenty to work with," he said, "but don't think you're bullshittin' me. You haven't told me half of what happened between you and these guys, but considering the shit the cops and DA pulled, I don't fuckin' care. Unless this does go to trial; then you'll tell me everything, abso-fuckin'-lutely everything that happened or I will not defend you. You got me?"

I nodded and winked at him. He leaned back, eyeing me.

"Y'know," he said, "suddenly I'm glad we're on the same side." Then he left.

They kept me in the hospital for another four days ("for observation," as Doug-deux put it) and the DA waited till the very last minute to do it, making it seem I'd wind up going from hospital jail to real jail, but as I was processing the medical paperwork and the basketball suit was readying his handcuffs word came down that all charges against me *had* been dropped, and I was free to go.

I thought I'd have to grab a cab home, but as I was wheeled into the hospital lobby, there were Joseph and Lonnie, waiting for me. Worried. Hopeful. Relieved at seeing me approach. Horrified at how damaged I still was. The second I saw them, I burst into tears. They embraced me and I bawled and then they drove me back to my condo.

And this time it didn't dare not let me cross the threshold.

Thirteen

The next few weeks I spent resting and drifting (this haze courtesy of Percocet) but I was never alone; Joseph moved into my guest room (one of the glories of being an IT guy is flexibility of workstation), and he saw that I was fed and had my bandages cleaned and tended to. And to my surprise, he purees chicken soup like nobody I've ever known.

What surprised me even more was, the more I saw of him, the more I saw in him. Not just his big beautiful eyes and classic profile, but how compact his body was – not muscular or buff but not unformed (if that makes any sense), he just looked...real – with hair in the exact right spots to add to his attractiveness. And then there was his gentle smile that could flash to impish without even a thought. And the moments he was so lost in a script job, this ethereal quality filled his face and enhanced everything about him. And the steadiness he offered me was something I hadn't realized could be so nice. I wondered at never having seen these qualities in him, before.

Lonnie came by, a few times, with the latest gossip...which I had to listen to since I couldn't tell him shut to up; I was wired for another four weeks, and it would take me months of therapy after that to get to where I was able to give the world's best blow jobs, again. Lonnie being Lonnie, he made the most of it (okay...like I'd ever been able to silence him when I *could* talk).

Chris even dropped in, once, and I did my best to assure him nothing that happened that night was in any way because of him. What's funny is, I was over him. Yes, he was beautiful. Still is. And I still think the way his hands mixed drinks bordered on poetry. But by the time he came,

I'd had my fill of saucer-deep boys who offered nothing more than their beauty. To prove all was well, once I was unencumbered by cast or wire, I took some photos of him and he used them to work his way into a decent modeling career. He's in New York, now, with his wife (not that having one means anything) and I smile when I see him in print for some major clothing designer...or walking a runway in nothing but a Speedo and his new tattoos. Still beautiful, and nothing more.

As for the boys, I deliberately avoided doing anything that could even conceivably lead back to me. That I never heard a word about the videos and what happened in that room in the lease bugged me, but I wasn't willing to check into it just yet – in case someone was hoping I'd expose my complicity in what happened and reveal to the world that I really WAS some dangerous faggot. It wasn't easy but I decided to put it all on hold till I was back to flexibility; maybe by then the uproar would be part of the forgotten past.

Oh, and was there an uproar. Initially, the local media reported it as a "Man Attacks Student At Knifepoint" kind of thing that shifted into "Fraternity Students Stalked By Deranged Homosexual" and "Judge's Son Threatened" then degenerated to "Homosexuals Out To Destroy Society" on the Opinion Page and commentaries by local pundits and politicians which lead to "Gay Men Attacked In Anti-Gay Rampage" (all written without reference to how the gay men fought back and sent their attackers running, according to Lonnie) and "Homosexual Male Arrested For Assault" (that being Owen, who had the audacity to beat the shit out of a guy who'd come at him with a crowbar; charges were quickly and quietly dropped, which was not reported on) and a few drive-by shootings at gay bars and businesses before the media finally got the idea that maybe, just maybe, they ought to stop fanning the flames of hate before somebody got killed.

Of course, that didn't stop the maniacs in their Sunday pulpits (church and TV) from continuing to deride "queers and liberals" as being the cause of America's fall from grace, nor did it prevent those devil worshipers from Kansas from dropping by to picket city hall with their "God Hates Fags" worship. I watched it all with a mixture of weary acceptance and awe at how many people deliberately refuse to think beyond the end of their nose while choosing to believe

139

anything that comes out of the mouth of the "right" person. Talk about sheep...though I'm certain if sheep had a voice they'd claim insult at the comparison.

But then a blogosphere reporter (who obviously hadn't gotten the memo that one only reports the version of events put forth by the police department or District Attorney's office) wrote about the attack on me and the near attack that Joseph and Owen had prevented. Of course, she was dissed by the mainstream media...until Udall began quietly spreading some gossip on his own. Soon after the whole tone began to shift.

By the end of the second week, noisy questions were being raised about one certain judge using his influence to protect his out-of-control frat-brat. And some wondered why the police and DA were refusing to investigate what was probably a series of hate crimes (they tied the attack on the two guys prior to mine to Reza's Mustang and even drew in Cameron's involvement in the near riot with that Latino family). And commented on how the gay community felt so threatened, they'd had to set up their own patrols for protection since the cops wouldn't do it. And suddenly I had a visit from Ms. "Thuffering-thuccotash."

She just showed up, unannounced, and all but threatened Joseph to make him let her in. Of course, she looked exactly like I expected – tall, willowy, short blond hair and carefully crafted makeup, the perfect business suit for court, comfortable but stylish pumps, a leather briefcase and the latest in designer purses – whose attitude screamed "young Republican."

I was resting, but when I heard it was her I cleaned up...then let Joseph "help me" into the living room to show her how badly hurt I still was. I put on quite a performance...and she couldn't help but notice the moldings on my arm and shoulder and the wires in my mouth. She went a bit whiter than she already was, even under her foundation and soft shade of blush.

"Mr. Preston, I – I didn't – ."

"Presslea," Joseph snapped. "And I'm not gonna correct you, again, lady."

"Mr. Presslea. I apologize. I've come to talk with you about your case."

140

I made a big show of how difficult it was to write with my left hand and asked, Which?

"The initial assault on you. My office now believes there is sufficient evidence to move forward with criminal charges against the young men who participated in your attack. It's my understanding you may have gathered more information concerning their involvement in not only your assault but the assaults on others. Have you anything you wish to share with me concerning this case?"

That you're a cowardly, homophobic, fucking cunt, hit my brain, but since I couldn't speak it stayed there. Dammit. I wrote out, What do you have already?

"Mostly circumstantial evidence, especially as regards the other two assaults. Of course, in the confrontation where Sanderson's windshield was shattered, the young men did nothing specifically illegal and, in fact, claim self-defense. But if we can try them for your assault, a conviction could be used to bolster our case." She looked at Joseph. "We also have your statement and the statement of another witness."

"Lonnie," said Joseph.

"Yes."

"He got part of a license plate number."

"Yes. And our initial search drew nothing...but then I noticed the clerk who'd input the information had inverted a couple of numbers. Once that was corrected, we tracked it to Judge Moretti's Ford Bronco. It was an unforgivable slip."

Meaning they'd found a way to excuse brushing me off, the scum.

She looked at me. "Now I hear you and Judge Moretti's son had an ongoing relationship. Is that correct?"

I nodded.

"Is it verifiable?"

I nodded.

"Is it possible you were using this attack on you to get even with him in some way?"

Panther roared. That fucking cunt. So they were going to turn this back on me, anyway.

I must have had some look on my face, because she quickly added, "I have to ask. Moretti's lawyer's already floating that as a defense strategy."

I wrote, Ask Chris, and gave her the bar's phone number. Now was the time to give out info that could be backed up. And Chris would tell her about how I'd picked the little shit up the night before he and his buddies jumped me. I also told her just enough about Jayson's ankle to get her interested.

"Excellent," she said. "This will help." She rose to go. "And please let me extend my deepest apologies, Mr. Presslea. What with the budget cuts and increases in crime, sometimes cases we don't feel a hundred percent sure of are shunted aside in favor of the proverbial slam-dunk. It's not right, but it is reality. I hope you'll be better soon."

I nodded and Joseph showed her to the door. I had him call Udall to relay the details of her visit. He laughed so hard, he couldn't talk. That made Panther purr.

The third week, I started back to work so I could ignore the nonsense. Well...looking for work. Wendahl had gotten wind of the uproar and sent me a kind letter thanking me for all I'd done for them, and would I please send all the relevant codes for the sites? For use by their new in-house IT guy? A nice way of saying, We don't want you, anymore. The same happened with two other companies I dealt with. But it didn't matter.

It was about here I began to wonder about shifting my focus to photography (pun intended). So using the shots I'd taken in Chicago and some artsy sessions of Lonnie and his paramedic (the cute, stocky compliment to Lonnie's lean & mean) I shot with a decent digital camera I bought, I built up a nice portfolio. I actually got my first commission from the state magazine asking for images of the gay community for a story they were planning about the uproar. With Lonnie's and Joseph's help, I shot more than two hundred images of demonstrations and meetings and bars and people on the sidewalk over the course of the fourth week. They used five of the twenty PFDs I sent for approval. Now I had a new direction in life...and I began to feel hopeful.

What brought me joy was, that's also the week Judge Moretti resigned his bench and returned to private practice. Udall dropped by to boast.

"He was being threatened with sanctions by the judicial board of review. And the Attorney General was considering investigating him for interfering with a criminal investigation. Little fuck took the easy way out."

By this point, I was able to mutter intelligibly, "What'd you expect? What kind of law does he practice?"

"Corporate. Like Winslow."

"I'll be sure not to invest in any company he's working for."

"Smart move," he laughed. "I hear his kid's been put in rehab."

"Really? He never struck me as a junky."

"Gay rehab. Some clinic in Kentucky, near Cincinnati."

YOWL! "That mother-fucking-son-of-a-bitch."

"What do you care about Freddy Moretti?"

"What I care about is, him and his father acting like my sexual orientation is something that can be treated and cured, like alcoholism or drug abuse. It's fucking insulting."

"He's fucking retarded, what can I say?" He eyed me. "You ever gonna tell me all the shit that happened?"

I dipped my lips in some water. "Do I have to?"

"I'd prefer to minimize the surprises." I just smiled. "Okay, then answer me one thing. How many times were you with the Moretti kid?"

I glared at him and snarled, "That 'kid' is twenty-one years old, which makes him an adult. A man. And I'll be thirty next month, not sixty."

"Point taken."

I drew in a deep breath, but Panther was still rumbling so I held up four fingers. Let Freddy prove otherwise.

Udall nodded and smiled.

"What about the other guys?" I asked.

He shrugged. "I didn't keep up on them. Now school's almost out and the university's considering revoking their charter for next year. Too much publicity of the negative kind."

I sighed. It was too bad that those five little shits killed it for the other fifty-five or so guys. I actually hoped they'd just be put on probation, and made a mental note to send the Chancellor a letter stating as much.

Udall wanted to chat some more, but my jaw and ribs were beginning to ache so I begged off. Besides, I had some thoughts spinning in my head about Freddy and gay rehab, and I wanted some peace to sort them out. I told Joseph I was lying down for a bit and closed the door to my room, then I sat by the window and let my mind drift.

I'd lied when I told Mika the info on his family was set to go out to immigration, but since I wound up in the hospital and couldn't do anything about anything, he probably thought it had happened and was running scared. And I felt...wrong about that. I tried to track down Anibal but hit a wall in Brasilia so had to let it go. I wished Mika the best.

As for the videos, I couldn't really do anything about those for at least another week. Question was, what would I do with them? It seems being knocked about even worse than before had altered my perspective, again.

I still had Panther in my heart, but now he was somewhat domesticated. More a tool in a box of capabilities that I could use as need be. But I now just wanted to stay under the radar. I seriously did not want any actions I took to come back on me or hurt Joseph in any way, form or fashion, even via guilt by association.

But the manifesto was boiling in my brain. Seriously on fire. Fucking Freddy was basically saying that being gay needed a twelve-step program, and his fucked up father was backing him up on it. Plus the other guys were apparently so ashamed of the fact that they had all gotten hard while having sex with a man, they were ignoring it – as if that would make it go away. Granted, what I'd done to three of them counted as rape, but still the two straightest of them had cum while being fucked, and Mika would have shot a load, too, if I'd sucked on his dick instead of going after Freddy's. They were proof positive of the idea that men are capable of sex on just about any occasion, so small wonder they were keeping quiet about it.

Which brought me back to a sort of reality. Many rape victims *are* so ashamed of what happened to them, they hide it and try to rebuild their lives on their own. Which is a diseased way of treating the problem but also one that is understandable considering how the world acts about sexual assault. There was a recent case of a porn star being raped in his apartment by a man he'd invited home. I saw photos of his injuries posted online and he talked about it in his blog, and half the comments were accusations he'd made it up. That he was lying. And many came from the gay community. It was brutal and vile, and also way too typical.

That realization calmed Panther down to where he wasn't yowling about Freddy, but he was still grumbling and angry and in need of some strokes.

So I sat at the window for an hour. Watched the traffic pass below. Silent. Almost like watching a TV on mute. We were having a cold spell to usher in June, rain mixed with a dash of sleet and sharp breezes cutting against the new leaves, and it looked right and elegant and real as people scurried about in their coats and umbrellas trying to keep from getting too wet and cold. And my mind danced around with the wind.

I realized I hadn't heard a word from my mother during all of this, which was not in the least bit surprising. She probably wasn't even in town, never being the sort who loves the cold. And from what I could tell, the story hadn't expanded much beyond the city limits, except in the blogosphere – but the only people who pay attention to them is those who want to argue or agree; the mainstream media still pretty much ignores them until forced to take notice. So it looked like my little episode would fade into the nothingness of history, without meaning or context or point or anything to make it worthwhile. That made Panther growl, again.

Suddenly I got up, went to my computer and opened it – and constructed a new blog. "My Porno Manifesto." And my first post was –

"I think it's time for people to admit that men were meant to be fucked. That's how they're built, physiologically. That's how they're wired, emotionally, whether they wish to admit it or not, since they think about little more than sex and it's not always available from a female. It's only the stupid, contrary teachings of bigots and fools who keep us from seeing this. And why do they do it? To keep us under their control? To give us somebody to hate? To make some people wrong so they can be right? Yes, to an extent. But I think ninety percent of the reason most societies denigrate and despise homosexual men and women is due to habit. That's what they were brought up to do, as were their parents and grandparents and ancestors leading back to some absurd passages in the bible or Talmud or something that was geared solely to giving authorities the right to codify the need for increasing the population by restricting male sexual activity to include the one member of the human race who could bear children, and if he used any other method for relief – be it his hand or a sheep or a man's ass – was damned to hellfire and ostracism and death. Period.

"Well – habits can be broken, and history can be revisited. And that is what my blog will do. From this day forward, let it be known that a man having sex with a man is normal and natural, and anyone who says otherwise is deliberately ignoring the truth of how men are put together. And I don't give a damn who they say they are. The fact is, any man, no matter how geared he is towards having sex with a woman, any man is capable of having sex with another man and achieving satisfaction from it.

"And I have more than enough proof."

Then I attached a video of Freddy and Jayson to the bottom of the post, and made myself a note to Google up some specific biological references to back up what my next post would be – dealing with the location of the prostate. Later would come posts about gay sex being nature's version of birth control along with discussions of the "gay-for-pay" phenomenon in porn, the Greek manner of education giving birth to Democracy (meaning America was founded on principles put forth by faggots, honey), sexual realities in prison and all boys schools, and the history of homophobia in western and eastern societies. Now Panther was purring with delight.

The following Friday, I was released of the wires and body molds and handed over to a physical therapist to learn how to use my jaw and arm, again. They didn't think it would take much work; I was in good shape and my neck and facial muscles were strong.

Gee, I wonder why?

Anyway, now I could go back to the lease and see what was left of my once great and glorious plan for revenge.

And the answer was, not much...but maybe just enough.

Fourteen

I waited till Tuesday, because first I had to slip away
from Joseph. Sometimes he'd fuss over me like a mother
partridge does her brood, though I'd grown to enjoy his low-
key bossiness. It actually made me feel safe and needed and
comfortable. But sometimes, especially around lunch and
dinner, he did hover a bit. Fortunately, that day he was
handling a problem for one of his own clients and was seated
cross-legged on his chair, meaning he would be deep into
techno-mode for the next three hours, at least. So I told him I
was going for a drive and he nodded at me with minimal
awareness, his expression child-like and innocent. The picture
he made, it brought tears to my eyes. I quickly snapped an
image of it...and he never noticed. I used to be able to
concentrate like that.

Of course, I'd left my car down the street from the
lease and had to ask Joseph and Lonnie to retrieve it, while I
was in the hospital. The reason I gave them for parking it
there was I couldn't find any other slot. Lonnie didn't buy it
but couldn't get any other story out of me so had to let it be. I
promised to buy them dinner at a steak house on Clarion
Street.

So I drove over and rounded the block twice before
stopping in front, all to make certain no one was watching the
place. I couldn't see anybody who looked suspicious – but
then, how would I know?

I parked down the street and slipped up to the house.
Its yard was overgrown and I noticed a postal form on the
front door; not a good sign. It told me I had a registered letter
from the realtor. Grandaddy's company must have found out

147

and canceled the lease. I tried my key; it worked, so I guess I'd come before they'd decided to initiate the eviction process.

I entered and looked around. The lights were still in place, as was the material I'd draped from the landing. Of course, Mika's clothing was gone, but my Pantax was still behind the material and the rolls of film hadn't been touched. Panther purred at that. I yanked the material down, packed away the lights and took everything to my car. Now I had to go upstairs.

The table was still there but the TV was gone, as were two of my cameras. I'd placed the micro-digital one in the ceiling light and pointed it straight down to the table, so I climbed up to find that it was still there. Cool.

When I got down off the table, I noticed stains on the floor around one end of the table. And the wood was scuffed. And the legs had odd scrapes, like someone had been rubbing rough cloth up and down them. None of that was from my session with Mika, so I checked the camera. Its battery was drained – which might prove interesting, since I'd set it to record when there was movement.

Next, I climbed up to the attic. The mainframe was right where I left it and it was on...and the relays from the frat house were still feeding into it. I'd removed the monitor so had no way of knowing, yet, when it had reached capacity, and I'd disabled the purge, so I knew it still had up to my last encounter with Freddy and the beating I took on it, at least. Panther leapt for joy. I powered it down, disconnected it and took everything downstairs.

I set everything in a pile by the door then went to a window to look across at the frat house. It was beginning to get dark and the place was quiet. Looked empty. I figured finals must be pretty much over, so the guys must have gone home. That or they were already tossed from campus.

I packed the camera and mainframe in my car and set the table out for trash. I should have just hopped in and driven away, but I got to thinking about the cameras and relays in the frat house and wondered if I could sneak in to get them. I was tired and achy – and part of me was screaming, No, get the hell away from here – but I wanted to be done with it, so I slipped into the back yard, snuck through the opening and scurried up to the kitchen door.

148

I looked inside. Saw the security monitor reflected on the fridge was glowing green, meaning it was off. Meaning the place wasn't empty, yet. Dammit.

"What're you doing here?!"

I jumped around to find the sweet kid from the kitchen glaring at me. He wore a short-sleeve collarless shirt and cargo shorts, revealing nice legs with sandals on his feet. But his sweetness was replaced by being really pissed off, and his voice sounded very East Coast.

"Sorry, I was – I, uh – ."

"You're the guy that did this."

Panther hissed. "Did what?"

"Our charter's been revoked. Happy, now?"

"No." And I meant it. But there were still growls from deep within. "I'm sorry."

"Are you?"

"I wrote the chancellor asking him not to punish everyone for the actions of a few jerks. Is there a chance you'll get your charter back, next year?"

"No. He thinks some of us knew what those jerks were doing and didn't stop it. Called it inappropriate behavior and very disappointing. I got a report in my file and a letter was sent to my folks. The only way they'll pay for college now is if I go to U-Mass so they can keep an eye on me. They don't believe I didn't know. I'm nineteen fuckin' years old, and they want to ground me, like I was twelve. All thanks to you."

"Me? I was the one gay-bashed."

"Cam said you were spying on us. That's why they went to beat you up – to warn you off."

"And you believe him?"

"What're you doin', now?"

I jolted. He had me, there.

He nodded to the back of the yard. "Is that how you'd get in? Through the fence? Sneak in so you can spy on our dicks? Or do you like asses?"

His snottiness irritated the fuck out me. Panther paced, like in a cage, growling a warning.

"Dicks," I snarled. "I love the look of 'em, and they're easy to get to. Asses are nice when I'm in the mood to fuck, but I'm always ready to suck on a beautiful cock. How's yours?"

"Just...get the fuck outta here, or I'll call security."

I started moving towards him. "Why? What are you scared of? What is it about me that makes you so afraid? That I might make a pass at you? That I might force you to let me suck you off? Or that I might fuck you? Or maybe you're afraid you might find out you like it. Just like Reza did. And Jayson. And Cameron. And even fuckin' Freddy."

He grabbed a log of firewood that was kept by the door and readied it as a weapon.

"Keep away from me!"

We were by the carport and the only cars left were a Honda and a Pontiac. Meaning he might not be alone. So I leaned against a post, smiling.

"I'm not going to touch you," I purred. "The other guys, they're the ones who attacked me. And Cameron Sanderson is lying. I'd never been here, before. I was just walking down the street when I was jumped."

"Bullshit! You act like my uncle, and nobody knows he's gay till he tells 'em, so how would they know you were?"

"Freddy." He eyed me, confused. "I met him, the night before. Took him home. And I gave him the best blow job of his life. And he thanked me by leading those other fucks to me."

"You're lying."

"You know where he is, now?"

"He – he left, a couple weeks ago. Dropped out."

"He's at a gay reparative clinic. To get 'straight'."

"Bullshit."

"No shit."

"How do you know?"

"That's where my attorney had to send a subpoena."

That stopped him short. "But – those things're bullshit. My uncle says all they do is fuck you up."

Suddenly Panther was seated and curious. I think I may have actually looked at this kid like a cat might eye something odd but not quite scary.

"Wait – you said your uncle's gay."

He nodded. "He got married during Spring Break. I was best man."

"U-Mass – you're from Massachusetts." He nodded. "And I ruined it for you, here. I'll do what I can to make it right."

"You can't. It's done."

He was right; it was. And suddenly I felt so very sad. "Y'know, it never would've happened if the police had just done their job. I wouldn't have felt like I had to take it on myself and...and..." My voice trailed off. My head pounded and jaw and arm ached and I was brutally tired.

The boy lowered the log. "So, you did this for revenge?"

I shook my head. "I did it to try and understand why. There's nothing wrong with me. I'm not sick. I'm not an aberration. I'm just like them and they're just like me. And so are you."

"I'm not queer."

Panther growled, again; he didn't like that word. I just whispered, "Nobody is, and everybody is. And I can prove it."

"With somebody else, okay?"

No, not okay. Panther was chittering. Looking this kid up and down like a he was a young gazelle that had wandered too far from the protective flock. Good legs. Nice ass. Pretty mouth. He'd be a fun, easy lunch.

I must have had some look on my face, because he backed away, a little.

"Please...just go. Don't make things worse than they already are."

Panther grew silent. The kid was right. He was one of the good guys, and to use him to prove my point would put me in the realm of evil. And even with as much growling and prowling as Panther had done, that was not where I wanted to go. So I figured in a week the house would be empty and I could take the cameras out then. I smiled at him.

"Give your uncle my best wishes," I said.

And I left.

151

Fifteen

When I got home, Joseph was beside himself.

"You were gone so long," he said. "I got worried."

"It felt so good to be out and about, again," I said, "I lost track of time. I picked us up some Korean barbecue."

"So my nose tells me. Feeling adventurous?"

"I'm sore, but I want to get back to chewing. I may still wind up asking for some puree."

"You'll be fine. I'll set the table." He jaunted into the kitchen, and watching him walk made my heart leap.

"How'd things go with your client?"

"I need to upload something from my desktop, at home."

"You ever going to show me where you live?"

He brought dishes and silverware in, grinning. "It's just a ratty loft in the warehouse district. But I like the space." He set the table, glancing at me as I laid out the food. "In fact, I was thinking – I can stay there, now."

I looked at him, startled. "Oh?"

"You're up and on your own, again. And my set-up's better there."

"I see. I – I'll miss you."

"Me hovering and bossing you around? All the time I've known you, you've lived on your own. I thought you'd be happy to get back to it. You have a lot that's secret in your life, Alec. And sometimes I feel like I'm in the way."

"No, Joseph..."

He jaunted into the kitchen and brought out some water.

"It's okay. It'll be nice to be home. And we'll still see each other at the bar."

I nodded, then added, "And other times. Right?"

"Careful, Alec. It's beginning to sound like you want to start dating."

I hesitated then said, "I wouldn't be against it."

He looked at me, sat at the table and portioned out some rice. I sat across from him and focused on the strips of spicy beef and asparagus.

"Alec," he finally said, "I like you, and think of you as a good friend."

Shit.

"You've been a better friend to me that I have to you."

"You said that before, and it's not true. You've always welcomed me. Never treated me like a geek."

"'Cause we're both geeks."

"No, we're not. Well, maybe you're the TV version of one while I'm the reality."

"Don't say that about yourself. Your hands are the most elegant – ."

"Okay, they come from Adonis. It's the rest of me that's Bottom."

"Bottom?"

"From 'A Midsummer Night's Dream.' He's the weaver who became a half-ass."

I chuckled. "But didn't some queen fall in love with him?"

"Titania, who was under a magic spell, until she woke up and went back to Oberon, her king. And forgot about Bottom." He focused on his food, for a moment, then continued, "I like being friends with you. I don't want to lose that."

"But, I – ."

"Alec – I don't want to lose that. When dinner's done, I'm heading home. And I'll see you at the bar, okay?"

I nodded and stopped chewing my food. My jaw was back to aching and my teeth weren't happy, either, so I said, "This wasn't such a good idea," and cut my bits of beef into tinier pieces so I could just swallow them. Same for the asparagus and the rest of the rice.

Joseph left after we'd done the dishes, and my condo suddenly seemed to have echoes. I sat and stared out my bedroom window for an hour then worked on my blog for a bit. I was starting to get comments – some serious, some interesting, some asshole-y – to my manifesto and I decided, No moderating. Let the world see how vile people get when their beliefs are challenged. It would prove interesting.

Then I unloaded the car and laid the equipment out. I hooked the mainframe up to my desktop and let it reboot as I set the digi-cam to recharging since I didn't have a backup battery. I eyed the rolls of film and wondered where to take them for developing. I knew how to process film but hadn't set up a darkroom. Still...the idea of doing it myself intrigued me. I decided to look into it, tomorrow.

By now the mainframe was available, so I went into it and pulled up the downloads. Sure enough, it had maxed out the memory so everything was very, *very* slow. I dumped two cameras' files, from the den and patio, and that helped a bit. I finally was able to watch the one in Freddy's bathroom and started with him and me.

He backed in and I followed, groping him. From above, he was like poetry. I sat on the toilet, felt him up some more and pulled out his dick. His eyes were closed but something I noticed was his hands were at his hips and his fingers were caressing the area where his thighs joined his torso. His dick was so fucking lovely from overhead, and my hands were all over his legs and then his balls and dick, to the point where it seemed like I was worshiping them. It went on for close to three minutes before Jayson barreled in and punched Freddy then began to pummel me. And that startled me.

I'd have sworn it was Cameron who hit me, first. But he never showed. Reza joined Jayson and helped him pound and kick and slam me about, and Jayson found the switchblade just before several other boys roared in, apparently shouting. They did nothing to stop them until the sweet kid shoved Reza off me and pushed Jayson away. Now I was glad I hadn't followed my inner critter.

I lay on the floor, not moving, and seeing it – I dunno, it was like what they say you see when you're dying; you drift up and watch everything from above. The sweet kid tended to me – I wish now I'd learned his name, but by the time I thought to track him down through the school's files,

154

they'd been locked down to where I'd have to leave a trail if I wanted to force my way in or take a week to figure out their new security system, and I just didn't feel up to it. Ten minutes later, paramedics arrived.

The other tapes showed Freddy seated on his bed, holding his face. Jayson talked with him and showed him the knife. Suddenly Freddy pointed at the bathroom and started trying to explain (damn me for not adding the sound option) and Reza came over to listen. But neither of them seemed to believe him. Not until the cops showed up; then Reza grabbed the switchblade and showed it to them. I could see the whole story playing out in just his movements and anger.

The faggot used this to rape my buddy. We found them and stopped him. Really ballsy of the queer, but they're like that, now. Yada, yada, yada.

But something else I noticed was how Jayson kept sending angry glances at Freddy, who seemed not to notice. Then Cameron came in and spoke with Jayson, who talked to Reza, who also cast Freddy a glare that spoke of pure hate. And after I'd been taken away and the police were gone and the place had quieted down, Jayson joined Reza in his room, with Cameron, and they had a long talk. Cameron must've gotten a good view of the videos.

I checked the cameras for Mika's room and saw Cameron help him inside. Mika was dressed and shaking. Cameron gave him a drink, something that looked like water but since there was so little of it I figured it for Vodka or Gin. Especially since Mika choked on it. When Cameron left, he went into his shower, stripped and washed himself for the next hour. When he was done, he wrapped himself in a towel, made a call on his cell phone then pulled out a suitcase and packed. Reza came in when he was almost done and spoke with him for a long time...and Mika finally wound up nodding. Reza left and Mika put the suitcase away and lay on his bed. He stayed there the rest of the night.

The picture he made – the towel covering him from knee to waist, legs crossed at the ankles, his hands behind his head, his eyes focused on the ceiling, his lips still quivering – it was lovely and painful. I was sorry for what I'd done to him – yet Panther still purred with the knowledge that I'd possessed someone so beautifully formed.

The mainframe carried the next day's activity in the boys' rooms – most of it straightforward – but something happened in the evening that caught my attention. First there was a meeting between Cameron, Reza, Mika and Jayson with Freddy in his room. They seemed to be nervous and were discussing something that angered them, then they filed out. Two hours later, Jayson came back to his room, packed his stuff and moved down to Mika's room. He seemed nervous and jerky in his movements.

I checked the cameras in Mika's, and he came in, changed from his usual board shorts and t-shirt into jeans, dress shirt and jacket, grabbed his suitcase and left before Jayson walked in. Reza wandered into his room and locked both doors. Then he sat on the floor and did not move for hours. Cameron strolled into his room and took a shower. He called into Reza's room, but Reza paid him no attention, so he flicked on his TV to watch some porn...then turned it off and stared at the ceiling.

Finally, Freddy staggered into his room and lay on his bed. Shirtless. In pain. By this time, Jayson was all moved into Mika's room and Mika was long gone. Then the mainframe reached its capacity and shut down. That left the digital camera.

I checked it. The battery was charged. I connected it to my computer and turned it on.

What I saw first was my rape of Mika, from overhead, and you could see everything, from the blood on his neck where I'd cut him to me entering him to the tears on his cheeks as he wept. And you could hear it – not great sound but good enough – and I was rougher and more brutal than I'd thought. In fact, I was shaken at the harshness of my voice and the animal-like grunts that came from within me. It also looked like he'd gotten harder than I remembered. And when I left him, he'd laid there for five minutes before he heard someone coming and bolted off the table.

The video then caught bits and pieces of Jayson, Cameron and Reza entering the room and storming about, but their voices were clear.

"Mika, you in here?" Reza entered and walked around. "These are his clothes."

"What the fuck's this?" Cameron snarled by the table.

"Dude, this is freaky," came from Jayson.

"Jays – Jays, those videos! What the fuck?"

Reza crossed near the table to look closer at the TV. He cried out.

Cameron grabbed him from across the table. "Motherfucker! That fuckin' happened? You fuckin' did that to me?"

I heard a struggle and Reza's strangled, "I thought you did it to me! He – he told me – ."

"Bullshit, you motherfuckin' faggot! You fuckin' ' – ."

"Guys, guys, guys, look!" That was Jayson. "You can see our rooms. And Freddy's – shit!"

Reza broke away from Cameron and the two of them joined Jayson. "It's that faggot!" Reza cried. "The one who – who – shit!"

He and Jayson bolted out the door. Cameron grabbed the laptop and slung it across the room. I heard it smash – then Cameron froze. "Mika?"

I heard Mika sobbing. "Don't tell them. Don't tell anybody. Please. Please, Cam."

"Dude, what happened?"

"Don't tell anybody. Please."

"Mika, buddy – buddy, c'mon, it'll be okay. C'mon. Put your pants on. Put 'em on. Okay, now your shirt. That's it."

"Don't tell anybody. Don't tell anybody."

"I won't. It'll be okay. Come on."

They left and the camera shut down. The next image was late at night when the light came on. Cameron lead Freddy into the room.

"I don't get it, Cam," said Freddy. "What's this got to do with that faggot?"

"Look out the window, man."

I caught a glimpse of Freddy passing. Heard more people come into the room.

"Holy shit," said Freddy. "He was spying on us?"

"You know fuckin' well he was," snapped Jayson.

"Bullshit! I didn't know anything about – ."

"I fuckin' SAW you, Freddy! He was feelin' you up and you were lettin' him!"

"He had a fuckin' knife!"

"In his pocket! I found it in his pocket! And it wasn't in his hand when he was – ."

"Why'd you pick him, Freddy?" This was Cameron talking, as he rounded the table. "You pointed him out to us, that night. Why him?"

"He was queer and it was in queertown."

"It wasn't the first time you saw him, was it?" asked Jayson. "You've been fuckin' around with him – ."

"Back off, Jays. You know fuckin' well that's not true!"

"No?" Holy shit, even Mika was there. "I have seen videos you helped him make."

"You made one of 'em look like you were fuckin' me!"

"I don't know what the fuck you're talking about!"

"You helped him get to us!" said Reza. "To me!"

Freddy started for the door, saying, "I'm out of here." Someone – probably Cameron – shoved him back on the table. "What the fuck!?"

"I talked to Michelle. She says guys who beat up on queers are usually queer. And they get other guys to go along to help hide it."

"Or to use for blackmail," said Mika.

"Guys, c'mon," said Freddy, scared. He was lying back on the table, watching one of them arc around him, his breath fast and his muscles tense. "I'm tellin' you, I don't know anything about this."

"And I seem to recall it being your idea to do it," Cameron continued.

"Bullshit, Cam! It was your idea!"

"I just talked about hating fags. You're the one made it into a contact sport."

"In all kinds of ways," said Jayson.

"Jays, you better fuckin' help me here."

"Or you'll what? Do to me what you did to Father Paul? Tell everybody he had you fuck him? Was that bullshit, too?"

"I saw the videos, Freddy," said Mika. "What you did to Jayson. What you helped that man do to Reza...and to Cam. He said I was to be next for you, but you gave me to him. Like I was a whore!"

"Now you're our whore, motherfucker," said Cam.

Freddy scrambled from the table, but I heard him get caught and struggle and cry for help until his screams were muffled. Then he was slammed face down atop the table, his t-shirt ripped away and used to gag him and tie his hands behind him. Reza and Jayson tied his legs to the table's legs with the rest of the shirt and held him down as Cam yanked his jeans and briefs down and stood back to let Mika take him, first. And the camera caught one of the most perfect shots ever as Mika worked himself up then shoved his dick deep into Freddy's perfect ass.

Freddy tried to scream but Reza held an arm around his mouth, muffling him even more. And Mika plunged away until he came inside him. He grunted and pulled out and some of his cum dribbled from the head of his dick, then he tucked himself away and took Reza's place so he could go next.

Reza took his time working himself up then pushing his long lovely dick into Freddy. He gripped Freddy's cheeks and slid in and out and in and out as if he was making certain the fuckee got the full benefit of the fucker. Then he began ramming harder and hard and gasped and shot his wad into Freddy. When he pulled out, it was Cameron's turn.

He was already set, but he felt the need to slap Freddy's ass a few times before he slipped in. By this point, it was easy to do and he humped the guy like he was a dog humping somebody's leg, a little sound like "mph-mph-mph-mph-mph" popping out of him. When he came, halfway into it he pulled out and let some cum shoot onto Freddy's naked back. Long lovely arcs of white fluid leaping from the tip of his dick to the nape of Freddy's neck. Then he switched places with Jayson...whose coke can of a dick was raging to go.

Freddy knew how big Jayson was, and he was fighting, again. Yanking at the ropes holding him and trying to avoid what he knew was about to enter him. It was no use. All he did was make his ass look even more inviting, the way it wiggled about. And when Jayson finally pressed against him, even as slick as the guy's hole was from three men's semen, he had to work it in. And Freddy screamed and fought the whole time. But once it was in there, it stayed. And Jayson really took his time.

What's interesting is, during the first three-fourths of the gangbanging of Freddy, Panther just watched. Purring, to be sure, but not vested in it. Yes, Mika, Reza and Cameron were lovely men, and the victim of their fucking was gorgeous, but I almost felt like I was watching a porno movie for which I had to write a critique. Until Jayson.

Because he crouched over Freddy. Almost covered him, completely. And his pants were down around his ankles, so his ass and legs were bare and clenching and quivering as he slammed in deeper and deeper. I began to wonder if he wanted to split Freddy in half, he was ramming so hard. And when he came, he pulled out to let it all fire onto Freddy's back and mingle with Cameron's cum. And the sight of him jerking on his own dick with more arcs of semen sailing across the beauty of Freddy's back. It made Panther growl and chitter like he'd just seen his dinner.

Once Jayson was tucked away, Reza cut Freddy's bindings and they left him lying across the table. He didn't move. Cameron leaned down to whisper something into his ear, so softly the mike didn't pick it up, but from his lips it seemed he was saying, "You tell anybody about this and you're dead." Then he gave Freddy's ass one last smack and they all exited the room.

Freddy lay there for another ten minutes before rousing himself and standing to pull his briefs and jeans back into place. His dick was anything but erect, but I noticed stains on the legs of his jeans. And I suddenly realized those stains on the floor – Freddy'd shot his wad while being fucked by his four buddies, and none of them had noticed. It was too perfect.

Freddy left and the image jumped to Cameron, Reza and Jayson clearing out the TV, cleaning away the remains of the laptop and finding the other two cameras. They worked silently except for one exchange as they unplugged the television.

"Which room?"

"The game room. That piece of shit we got in it now..."

"Yeah."

So they put my TV in their game room, probably to hook up to video games. If the frat had still been viable, I'd have sent them a copy of the game I'd just worked up. That'd be fun, when they saw what happened to the Avatar via the Minotaur. Not that I cared about the TV (I'd bought it through Granddaddy's company), I was just pissed about the laptop. Now I'd have to replace it and all the programs on it.

But the trade was worth it, oh was it ever.

Sixteen

The thing is, seeing that video made Panther hungry. Watching sex while not participating is like watching someone eat a banquet as you nibble on a peanut butter sandwich. It was worse than unsatisfying. It was infuriating. And it made me pace my lair, like I was caged, trying to figure out how to satisfy it.

I got in my car and started driving. Heading no place in particular. Just driving through the dark empty streets. I wound up near the campus and half thought about prowling back to the frat house to see if the sweet kid was still there, but I still felt that was not right. So I drove over to the working class section of town and spotted a couple of guys lounging around and looking available, but they looked dirty and dead of brain, and I wanted more than just my lips on some trick's diseased dick or to fuck some barely-wiped ass; I wanted a five course meal, front, back and top down to the tits and toes.

Still...one caught my eye. A near Woody clone, though with shaggier hair and the hint of a tummy, and a more dangerous glare. He wore a torn tee and tight jeans with holes at the knees and under his inviting ass, and his arms looked ready for mean, and the vision of him standing by a wall on one leg, the other foot cocked against the bricks to make him look oh-so-very-cool, made Panther growl with anticipation. He'd be fun to take down.

I still had Reza's Roofie, and I'd bought a six-pack of okay beer. It wouldn't take much effort to pop a top for him and slip the pill in without being noticed. Do a Soccer on him, all by myself in the back of my car. It'd be fantastic. Panther all but purred at the notion.

162

So I rounded the block, again. Telling myself I just wanted another look. And saw him eye me back. And then an SUV pulled up ahead of me and honked at him and he casually strode over and got in. Dammit. Now Panther roared in frustration – then settled back, confused.

I'd really been considering taking some hustler off the street, doping him up and fucking him? Was that stupid or what? Can you imagine what sorts of diseases you might get from that? Better to go for something clean and unused.

And suddenly I hit the brakes. I'd really been thinking about rape as a viable form of sex. And telling myself to make sure and use someone who'd never been with a man, before. Whether he wanted to or not. And the thought made me ill.

Panther was still in me, no question, but a new sense of right and wrong had set up shop next to him, and it was slapping my psyche around, viciously. I hadn't noticed it when I spoke to the sweet kid, but now I knew to take someone like an animal was way out of the realm of nice, and that's not what I wanted.

That's when I found myself driving through the warehouse district. I knew Joseph's address so input it into my GPS and found I was just two blocks from his loft. So I drove there.

It was a compact, brick, industrial building from the Twenties with big windows and twelve foot ceilings. I parked in the fenced-in lot next to it and rang Joseph's buzzer, hoping he was still awake.

"Who is it?" His voice held nothing but alertness.

"Alec. Can I come up?"

He buzzed me in. I rode an industrial elevator to the top. It opened into a loft that covered the whole damn floor and was done in the coolest of coolness – all simple and clean and functional and perfect. Joseph was there in a robe, waiting for me, looking like he was fresh out of the shower. Suddenly he reminded me of that adorable little weasel who caused so much mischief on a recent Sci-Fi series, with his longish hair dripping around his puppy-dog expression. I caught my breath at the loveliness of him...and the sexiness.

"What's wrong? Your voice is so – ."

163

Without a word, I embraced him. Held him as close as I could without crushing him. He was warmth personified. He was strength at its most supple. He was power. He was safety. He was home.

"Alec, are you all right?"

I buried my face in his neck. Loved the wetness of it. Smelled the hints of soap and shampoo it brought me. I rubbed his back.

"Can I stay with you?"

"Alec, is something wrong?"

I kissed his neck. Nuzzled his ear. Caressed his back with my fingers. He tried to pull away, but I wouldn't let him.

"Don't do this...Alec, please..."

"It won't just be tonight," I whispered. "It won't end till you end it."

I kissed him. He'd just brushed his teeth. The mintiness made my heart leap with joy. Panther was purring, but in that growly, happy way a cat gets when it's near ecstasy but not yet to the brink of opening the claws. I was not going to be denied.

I ran my hands through his hair. Backed him to a wall and crushed against him. Ground my crotch against his. Held him in place as I kept kissing him. He was starting to respond.

"Alec, no."

"I need you."

He pulled back, a little. "You don't know what you're doing."

"I want you."

He looked at me, startled. His big beautiful eyes wary, close to unwilling. I kissed one then the other. Pulled the robe away from his shoulders to let it drop. Then kissed down his neck to his tits and lingered on them. Sucking and kissing and nibbling and tonguing, bringing little gasps from him, before I continued down to his navel to his pubes. Holding his hands at his sides the whole time, so he couldn't get away. He began to breath heavily.

I flicked my tongue through his pubes and around his dick. It bumped against my cheek. I pulled back to view it for the first time...and it was poetry. Not as big as Woody or as perfect as Freddy or even a wonderful as Calvin, but it was

164

beautifully formed, elegantly curved and ready for me to use.
I tried to work my lips over it but couldn't open my mouth far
enough, yet, so I slipped my tongue and lips up one side and
down the other, pausing at the head to circle it. He moaned.

No more need to hold him in place.

I cupped his balls and rolled them gently in my hand.
They were round and full and felt just right. The hair on his
legs tickled my fingers. My other hand glided up the back of
his right leg to whisper over his cute little rear. It felt smooth
as a baby's bottom, so I turned him to face the wall to gaze
upon it...and suddenly Cameron's bubble butt and Reza's
perfect ass seemed gross and ungainly in comparison.
Joseph's back sloped into his cheeks with a gentle curve that
glided into a roundness that fit atop his legs so elegantly, I
could not have designed it better. Dimples to each side of the
line of his spine only seemed to emphasize how exact
everything was. I kissed each cheek. Nuzzled them. Rubbed
my face against them.

He giggled. "Cheek to cheek."

I stood and slipped my arms around him, one hand to
toy with his pubes, the other to tickle a tit. He leaned into me.

"Alec." His voice was deep. Husky.

I turned him to me and kissed him. He kissed me
back.

Then he whispered, "It's up to you."

I nearly swooned. A bit melodrama theater of a
phrase but the absolute truth.

Somehow we wound up on his bed in a room as
elegant as the rest of his place. I spent an hour worshiping
every square inch of his body with my lips and fingers before I
even thought about undressing. Then just before he could lose
control, I slipped off my clothes and lay atop him. Let my
dick rub against his as I kissed his lips and neck and tits. He
wrapped his arms around me, digging his nails into my back.
The feel of it all just about made me insane. I shifted and
grabbed his ass with both hands, parting his legs, kissing him
deeper and deeper.

He finally broke away and gasped, "Please...please..."

"Do you have a condom?"

He motioned vaguely to a night table. I reached over
and opened the draw to find a pile of various types. Probably

165

taken from the bars in hopes that were soon to be dashed. Well, never again, Joseph. Never again.

I pulled out two, slipped one onto myself and raised his legs to where they rested on my shoulders.

"You – your collarbone..." he whispered.

In answer, I used my spit to lube him and myself, then pressed the head of my dick against his hole. He tensed then wrapped his hands around my ass. I entered him, slowly. Gently. Carefully. Lovingly. Right up to where I could feel his ass against my hips. It was an exact fit.

Then I slowly began to slip in and out and in and out and in and out, letting him settle into his own rhythm. And in moments he was working with me, his muscles clenching and releasing and pumping in ways I'd never known possible, the expressions on his face almost painful in their obvious pleasure. He shifted his hands to play with my tits, sending screaming lightning from them to my ass and into my balls. It seemed like mere seconds before I was firing into him and oh...my...fucking...god, was the sensation overwhelming. I felt like I'd slipped underwater and was drowning in pure ecstasy. I almost wanted to cry...and may have had tears in my eyes, because Joseph touched them with his elegant hands, and I kissed his palms, one after the other. Then I lay atop him, still in him, unwilling to let go.

I finally rolled off to lay beside him. He was staring at the ceiling, almost in shock. I noticed his dick was softening and that he hadn't cum. Kissed him and whispered, "Oh, no you don't."

He looked at me, then I slipped down to work on him as best I could with my lips. In moments, he was hard, again. Using my tongue to lube him, I rolled the other condom onto him, inch by inch. Then I embraced him and rolled us over to where he was on top of me. He gazed at me, almost in awe. I grinned and pinched his tits. He shifted my legs up and slipped inside me, just as gently as I had with him. And the feel of him, the size and the fullness and the warmth of him, I could already tell I'd be letting loose, again.

He slipped in and out of me. Using shorter strokes that were more definite, in some way. And I ran my hands over his body. Over his arms. Over his face. Over his ass. And the strokes quickly became deeper and more intense and overpowering in the sensations they sent through me. And I felt Panther stir and growl and I pushed harder against him and dug my fingers into his ass and pulled at him and he cried out and let loose and fell atop me and embraced me with a passion I never knew possible as he plunged and fired and ground in as deep as he could as he came and came and I fired my second load all over me and him and even the headboard and laughed from the beauty of it all...and then burst into sobs.

It took him a moment to realize what I was doing, and he was still shaky when he said, "Alec?"

I wrapped my arms around him and held him close. Kissed him all over his face and ears, even as tears streamed from my eyes. Refused to let him go. I wanted him to stay inside me, forever. Because for the first time since Carson, I felt like I'd had more than just sex with another man...I felt like I'd made love.

And I never wanted to let it go.

Seventeen

So I didn't. Joseph and I saw each other nearly every night for the next three months, then I moved into his loft and sold my condo. Because of the area, I got a decent price for it, and I've lived off that and occasional I-T jobs for the last two years as I worked on my photography.

I started out taking photos of Joseph's hands and feet, they were so perfectly shaped. So exactly right. Shot roll after roll of them and wound up with a couple I actually had palladium prints made of. I sold them on-line for a nice price.

I retrieved my cameras and relays from the frat house two weeks later, without a bit of trouble; the place was up for sale so the security system was down. I was sorry for that; I now know Freddy approached others in the frat who didn't join in with his gay-bashing plans, so that gave me some hope...even though the little shits didn't stop him, either. And there was a story circulating on the gay blogs about the son of a high-profile judge walking away from a gay reparative facility and becoming a "gay-for-pay" porn star, but Panther didn't care if the story was true, so I made the deliberate decision not to find out.

The other guys just vanished into their own obscurity, and I felt that was good. The only one I still wonder about is Mika. It's weird, but even though I'm not the least bit sorry for raping him, I still hope he and his family turned out all right. And his pictures – most were just okay, but some are haunting in how they captured his defiant fear. I kept them secret, even from Joseph, until I was ready to show them to the world.

Lonnie and his paramedic are still together and having fun in their silly bondage games. Sometimes Lonnie even tells me in detail what they do; I think he figures being with Joseph is boring and maybe I'd like to join him for some of life's spice. I just smile and Panther purrs, listening with half an ear as if being scratched behind it. What Lonnie knew about the spice of life could be written on his pinky in letters ten feet high.

As for my manifesto – I actually caught a pundit on some Sunday show talking about it, derisively, which was a good thing. After that, hits on my blog multiplied times a hundred. And some commenters argue and others argue back and I've had to shut down a couple of flame sessions (and crash the mainframe of an asshole in Russia who thought he could crash me) and it's been royal fun.

So far I've written in depth about the ecstasy any man can achieve with anal sex, thanks to the prostate being located in just the right spot for a dick to massage. Referred to it as the male clitoris. And pointed out the anus is very flexible and noted that sex between men has been around since people began communicating and even expanded upon how the anal passage is the same shape as a dick. And did that start some great screaming bouts? To my intense pleasure I can say, abso-fuckin'-lutely, and not just from the right-wing-nuts who hate anything they don't like (that makes sense, just think about), but also from the female Dworkin freaks who think all men are scum and all sex is rape except when self inflicted.

I also got those two groups flaming each other (and me, of course) with a post about "gay-for-pay" porn and how just because the guys in it are fucking each other, that doesn't mean they want to give up women. My final point was that sex was being overly-simplified to fit a political agenda on both sides and they should just shut the fuck up about who's gay and who's not and let people fuck whomever they want without the sports commentary. And I posted the video of me and Reza with Ballerina to back it up. I got a call from the cops on that one. Somebody told them it looked like the girl was drugged, but since no one had filed a complaint, nothing was done.

So now Panther is content and happy, though every now and then he growls when he hears some twit say something rude about queers. But I haven't had to feed him anything more than Joseph.

The poor guy. I've taken so many of pictures of him, he now hides when I even look at my camera. But every one of them shows me a new facet in his expressions or sighs or stances, and I feel they help me get a little bit closer to him. In defense, he's begun taking pictures of me and he's so cute doing it, outside of the bedroom those moments are the purest joy.

I love him so much.

Now I'm prepping for my first showing in a gallery. It's next month and half the pictures are of him. The rest are a mixture of Lonnie, Chris, Freddy and Jayson (and fuck the consequences), the guy from floor 38 in Chicago and various shots from around the town. As well as two brutally haunting ones of Mika. And life is exactly where I want it.

And to those who might be shocked at my lack of repentance over what I've done, all I can do is shrug. Yes, I'm a man and I do know what is right and wrong in this world, and by some people's views what I did was evil and the fact that I don't care should be crushing; but I'm also an animal, and animals do not think in terms like that...not when they've been wounded. Then any reaction is honest and real.

Because that's how it's gonna be, from now on – when you push me, I'll push back. When you hit me, I'll hit back. When you hurt me, I'll hurt back. When you lie about me, I'll tell the brutal truth about you. When you use history or religion to say I'm wrong, I'll use science to prove I'm not. And I'll use every tool at my disposal, from blogs to the courts to baseball bats to forcing you to watch gay porn made by straight men with wives and babies at home till you want to yank on your own dicks and cum in your pants. And I'll keep at it till you acknowledge that I am just as normal as you are. So if you don't want Panther to bring out the claws, again, leave me and mine the fuck alone.

And that's what my manifesto is all about.

Kyle Michel Sullivan is an award-winning writer whose sole purpose in life is to tell stories that make his characters more real than the people he actually knows. After all, only fictional humans can truly understand him and be willing to talk to him at any time he wishes. He also sketches and paints and dreams of making movies.

CPSIA information can be obtained at www.ICGtesting.com
Printed in the USA
LVOW10s1646210615

443296LV00031B/1028/P